Kenyon jog...

The beagle was...
keep slack on th...
was in weapons...
a strong scent. And Kenyon needed to find his son.

They'd woven through the campground, not seeing the dark sedan anywhere. No sign of the car the kidnapper had been driving. He'd trust Peanut's nose over his own observations, though.

Suddenly, Peanut pulled hard on the lead, then sat down outside a cabin that appeared unoccupied. The curtains were drawn. When he tried the door, it was locked.

Kenyon bent toward the beagle. "Are you sure?"

The K-9 remained sitting with her nose in the air. Zach and his K-9, Amber, arrived. Amber sat down, as well, alerting.

"Looks like the dogs think this is the one," Kenyon said. "Door is locked."

* * *

DAKOTA K-9 UNIT

Ever since she found the Nancy Drew books with the pink covers in the country school library, **Sharon Dunn** has loved mystery and suspense. In 2014, she lost her beloved husband of nearly twenty-seven years to cancer. She has three grown children. When she is not writing, she enjoys reading, sewing and walks. She loves to hear from readers. You can contact her via her website at sharondunnbooks.net.

Books by Sharon Dunn

Love Inspired Suspense

Alaskan Christmas Target
Undercover Mountain Pursuit
Crime Scene Cover-Up
Christmas Hostage
Montana Cold Case Conspiracy
Montana Witness Chase
Kidnapped in Montana
Defending the Child
Targeted Montana Witness

Alaska K-9 Unit

Undercover Mission

Pacific Northwest K-9 Unit

Threat Detection

Mountain Country K-9 Unit

Tracing a Killer

Dakota K-9 Unit

Double Protection Duty

Visit the Author Profile page at LoveInspired.com for more titles.

DOUBLE PROTECTION DUTY

SHARON DUNN

LOVE INSPIRED SUSPENSE
INSPIRATIONAL ROMANCE

Special thanks and acknowledgment are given to Sharon Dunn
for her contribution to the Dakota K-9 Unit miniseries.

LOVE INSPIRED® SUSPENSE
INSPIRATIONAL ROMANCE

Recycling programs
for this product may
not exist in your area.

ISBN-13: 978-1-335-95727-6

Double Protection Duty

Copyright © 2025 by Harlequin Enterprises ULC

Love Inspired
22 Adelaide St. West, 41st Floor
Toronto, Ontario M5H 4E3, Canada
www.LoveInspired.com

Printed in Lithuania

MIX
Paper | Supporting
responsible forestry
FSC® C021394

But though he cause grief, yet will he have compassion according to the multitude of his mercies.
—*Lamentations* 3:32

For Charlotte...so glad you are in my life.

ONE

Raina McCord felt the small soft hand in hers for only a second before three-year-old Austin ran ahead of her. He chased his twin brother, Beacon, toward the elevator that would take them back up to the surface after having toured Wind Cave National Park. The boys had been so excited to come here. It was a beautiful day—unseasonably warm for October in South Dakota—and she'd loved seeing their excitement as they'd toured the vast underground network of cave passages. Now it was time to head back up and get the boys something to eat.

Raina narrowed in on Austin's dark head bobbing up and down as she tried to catch up with him. "Boys, wait for me, please!" she called.

A crowd had already gathered at the elevator doors, though they had just closed, transporting the first group from the cave to the visitor center. An adult stepped in front of Raina, blocking her view of Austin.

She pushed her way through, spotting Austin's dark head, but Beacon was nowhere in sight. She took a few steps and bent forward, cupping Austin's shoulder and speaking into his ear. "Where did your brother go?"

Austin pointed. "He got on the elevator."

Raina's heart beat a little faster as she stared at the closed door. Being separated from the boy who'd been her charge for the last nine months made her anxious. Ever since their widowed father—her best friend, Kenyon Graves—had been presumed dead, she'd been the twins' legal guardian. Kenyon had since returned home, amidst many tears of joy.

She glanced over her shoulder to look for Kenyon. She couldn't see him. He must have been pushed back by the crowd.

The elevator doors had closed just seconds before. It would take a while for them to travel the 108 feet to the surface. She prayed that Beacon would know to wait for them by the elevator doors.

A warm hand pressed on her back. "What's going on?"

She turned to face the twins' father. Kenyon had the same dark hair and blue eyes as his sons.

Her throat had gone tight from panic. "Beacon got on the elevator with the first group. He probably thought we were behind him."

Kenyon's only reaction was a slight lift of his eyebrow. "I'm sure he'll stay put once he realizes we didn't get on too."

She appreciated his calm response, which helped douse her fear. His steady reaction was probably a habit that came with his job as a detective for the Plains City PD. Only she could pick up on the slight waver in his voice that suggested he was more worried than he let on. Being able to read Kenyon came from years of them having been friends. She'd been ready to step in and raise his boys, despite the shock and grief she'd faced upon being told her friend was gone.

Nine months ago, Kenyon had been in an explosion while investigating a gun trafficking ring that was moving stockpiles of weapons across South and North Dakota. His body wasn't found, and he was presumed dead. His will had stipulated that she would become guardian to his children, and she'd started the paperwork to adopt the twins. Over a month ago, Kenyon had surfaced, only with no memory of what had happened or who he was. Work with a memory specialist had rehabilitated him to a degree from the trauma-induced amnesia. He continued to have blank spots in his memory that she tried to help fill in, and he was still readjusting to the life he had before the explosion.

She tried to remain calm as. "He'll probably ask a ranger for help once he gets out of the elevator." Beacon was a smart kid, but the boys were just shy of four years old. So young. She combed her fingers through her long red hair. "I talked with the boys about this sort of thing. What to do if they ever got separated from me. He'll know to wait for us." Did she sound like she was trying to convince herself that everything would be all right?

Austin tugged on her shirt hem. She turned and took his hand, holding it tight. Kenyon moved in closer to her as the crowd squeezed toward the elevator at the sound of it coming back down.

With Kenyon close, his strength and calmness permeated the air around her and helped her to take a deep breath. They'd known each other most of their lives. They'd always been best friends, nothing more. Except for in the past few weeks, when they'd been co-parenting his boys. The situation had become…awkward, to say the least. She'd been thrilled by Kenyon's return. But she'd been raising his kids for months and loved them more every day. What was her role in Kenyon's life now? Co-parent? Best friend? She was still staying in his guest room to avoid disrupting the boys' lives further. But they needed to have a serious talk about what would happen next.

When the elevator doors opened, they were among the

first to step inside. More people got in until the elevator was crammed full. She held on to Austin's hand and drew his head close to her side with the other hand. As people pressed in around her, she stared at the backs of their heads, scanning the tiny space and then the ceiling. This was the longest elevator ride of her life. Kenyon stood on the other side of her close enough that his shoulder touched hers. She tried to quiet her racing thoughts with a prayer.

Please God, let Beacon be okay.

She wondered if this was what a mom felt. She'd seen the women in stores whose children had vanished only to be found hiding under a clothing rack minutes later. She wondered now if she had that same look of stricken panic. But she wasn't the boys' mother. The twins had lost their mother, Monique, when they were barely a year old. She'd been happy when Kenyon had married Monique and the twins were born, and she'd been glad to help and be a support when cancer took his wife. After all, Kenyon had gotten her through the death of her parents when she was nineteen. He'd been her closest friend ever since.

Recently, he'd been cleared to go back to work. In fact, he'd joined the task force that was on the trail of the gun trafficking ring responsible for the warehouse explosion. The Dakota Gun Task Force, formed shortly after, aimed to take down the deadly traffickers.

She didn't want to put pressure on Kenyon with a difficult conversation. He'd been through so much already, but since his return, she couldn't help but feel anxious about what her status with the twins and with him really was or what it would become.

The smooth hum of the elevator and hushed conversation of the people around her did not soothe the fears that encroached on her thoughts about Beacon.

We don't know anything yet.

They elevator doors opened. Her body tensed as they waited for the people at the front of the elevator to get off. Both she and Kenyon were holding Austin's hands as they stepped out.

People milled around the visitor center. She scanned the entire area, not seeing any sign of Beacon. She took in a breath, trying to quell the rising panic.

Kenyon pointed toward a female ranger standing outside the gift shop. "I'll ask."

Austin squeezed her hand and shook his head. "Where is he?"

She bent down and gathered him into her arms. "He's got to be around here somewhere."

She watched as Kenyon pointed back toward Austin and then the ranger shook her head. Kenyon headed toward the restroom to search there.

She struggled to get a deep breath. It felt like an anvil had been placed on her chest. She milled past the clusters of people until she saw a man she recognized from the tour. They had spoken briefly while they were underground when he commented that he was a twin too.

"Excuse me. Were you on the first elevator up?" she asked the man.

"No." The man shook his head. "I came up in the second bunch. I was toward the front of the elevator."

That's why she hadn't noticed him. "Have you seen Austin's brother?"

He thought for a moment. "You know, as I stepped out of the elevator, I noticed a dark-haired little kid with a lady— they were headed for the exit door. I only saw them from the back. I just assumed it was you since the boy looked like one of the twins. I can't say if she had red hair like you or not. She had a hat on. Just saw them for a second."

Her heart beat a little faster. "Which door did they go out of?"

The man pointed to a door on the left. "Is everything okay?"

Her attention was drawn to Kenyon coming out of the restroom before she could answer the man. Kenyon shook his head when he saw Raina. She hurried over to him. "That man said he saw a woman with a dark-haired boy go out that door. It had to have only been a few minutes ago."

"That leads to the parking lot." Kenyon darted toward the exit.

Still holding Austin, she moved slower but followed Kenyon. Austin held on to her collar. She stepped out and the October chill permeated her skin. The fear she'd kept at bay bombarded her. Her mind raced in ten different directions at once.

Her heart pounded as a new wave of terror washed over her.

What if Beacon had been kidnapped?

Kenyon Graves raced into the parking lot, scanning the rows of cars. His son was missing, possibly kidnapped. He almost couldn't wrap his mind around the concept.

This can't be. Not after everything that's happened.

He kept running.

Please God, help me find Beacon. Keep him safe.

The thought of anything happening to his son created knots in his stomach. His boys had already been through so much in their short lives—losing their mother, then being told they'd lost their dad too. He had to find Beacon and make sure his son was all right.

He scanned the parking lot, tuning his ears to sounds around him. They had been only a few minutes behind the elevator Beacon had gotten onto. The kidnapper would have needed time to convince Beacon to go with her without raising a fuss. The woman could not have pulled out of the parking lot that fast. He lifted his head to see above some of the higher vehicles.

Raina caught up with him.

"Get to the car," he instructed. "Be ready. She has to be here somewhere."

Raina nodded and, still carrying Austin, hurried toward where they'd parked. He ran the width of the lot. A car pulled in not too far from where Raina was loading Austin into his seat.

Then he heard a scream that sounded like it had gotten cut off. A door slammed. He honed in on where the noise had come from and ran toward it. A dark colored sedan pulled out of a space. A woman was behind the wheel. One of the back doors on the sedan was a lighter color from the rest of the car.

Shock spread across the woman's face as she gunned the engine and headed straight for him. He jumped out of the way landing on his side on the asphalt. Waves of pain radiated through him as he heard the sound of squealing tires.

Raina pulled up moments later in his car. She opened the door. "I saw what happened. That driver meant to kill you."

She scooted across the seat as he pushed himself to his feet and got behind the wheel of the running car.

Austin was in the back in his car seat. Their pet beagle, Chewy, and Kenyon's K-9, Peanut, sat on either side of the car seat. Peanut was trained to sniff out guns and explosives. While Chewy occupied himself with his toy, Peanut seemed to know that something was wrong. She sat at attention and watched Kenyon as if waiting for a command.

The empty car seat next to Austin's made his throat go tight. He'd been separated from his sons for the better part of the year, after the explosion that had robbed him of his memory and precious time with his boys. He'd spent months wandering ranch land near his hometown, looking for work and unable to remember who he was or what had happened to him. He'd do everything in his power to make sure he was never separated from his sons again.

He drew his attention to the road as they pulled out of the parking lot and sped up. The car had a bit of a head start on them. He rounded a curve and the sedan came into view. The car wasn't moving at an excessive speed. Maybe the driver didn't want to call attention to herself or be stopped for speeding. Even though he hadn't seen Beacon in the car, the fact that he'd nearly been run over indicated that the woman was the kidnapper.

He pulled his phone out and handed it to Raina. "Call Daniel Slater." Daniel, a supervisory ATF agent and his boss on the Dakota Gun Task Force, would be able to help. "He told me this morning that he and Deputy Kelcey wouldn't be far from here investigating a lead connected to our trafficking case." Zach Kelcey was another member of the task force, a sheriff's deputy from Keystone. The task force had been formed from various K-9 law enforcement officers across the Dakotas. "Zach and his K-9 have a reputation for being able to find missing children. They'll be able to help."

She held the phone. "What should I say?"

A lump formed in Kenyon's throat. "Tell them that I am in pursuit of a dark sedan with a mismatched back door headed east in Wind Cave National Park for a possible kidnapping." He almost couldn't get the final words out. His mouth was dry. "Say that it's my son."

Raina nodded. She stared at the phone for a moment, her mouth drawn into a tight line, before pressing the number to connect. She reached over and padded his knee as if to reassure him.

"Say we need to put out an Amber Alert. They'll know what to do."

"I can do that." He could hear the phone ringing as she held it close to her face.

He was so glad she was here with him. She'd always been there for him. She'd always been there for his boys too. When Monique died, she'd supported his family. And when Kenyon was thought to be dead, she'd moved in and cared for his boys with the love and tenderness they needed. He didn't know what he would do without a best friend like her.

As the road grew curvier, he lost sight of the sedan.

He listened to Raina explain to Daniel what was going on while he watched the road, driving past open prairie and buffalo in the distance. Traffic coming into the park was fairly heavy, but not that many were leaving the park. It was still early in the day, not even lunchtime yet. There was only one car ahead of him, and it was light colored. He couldn't pass on the double yellow line. The road was curvy enough that the dark sedan might just be a little ahead of them but not visible.

Raina hung up. "You were right. They're not too far from here. They're on their way."

Raina turned in her seat to face Austin. "Hey, buddy, how are you doing?"

Austin kicked his feet. "Where's Beacon? Where are we going?"

The angst in Austin's voice was like a knife through his

chest. He caught a glimpse of his son in the rearview mirror, blue eyes clouded with confusion.

Peanut leaned closer to Austin and licked his face.

Raina undid her seat belt and stretched back even farther so she could squeeze Austin's foot. "We're not sure what's going on." She glanced nervously at Kenyon and then back at the boy. "But we're going to work real hard to find Beacon."

"Okay." Austin's voice sounded so fragile.

Raina dug through the bag she kept at her feet. "Why don't you have a sip of your juice box, Austin?"

He appreciated the calming effect Raina had on his son. Why she had never met someone and had kids of her own had always been a mystery to him.

"Thank you," said Austin.

The sweet soft voice so filled with trust made his chest tight. He was having a hard time getting a deep breath.

Raina turned back around and buckled in. She laced her fingers together in her lap as she stared through the windshield. Her jaw was tight and hard.

They drove toward the park entrance. The road straightened out. He glanced to the east.

"There, I see the car." Raina pointed at the part of the crossroads that led west. "She turned on the road that leads toward town." Hot Springs, the nearest town, was ten miles away.

He hadn't seen the dark sedan. The bunch of trees that grew along the road about fifty yards from the entrance could be blocking his view. He'd trust Raina's eyes. When he got to the park entrance, he hit his blinker and turned.

Kenyon handed his phone back over to her. "Let Daniel and Zach know which way we're headed."

Kenyon sped up. Raina's voice became background noise

to his own thoughts as she spoke to his colleagues on the task force. A parade of police reports and crime scene photos of bad things happening to children marched through his head. Memories of the calls he'd handled when he'd been on patrol as a rookie cop bombarded him.

He'd lost his wife. He could not fathom losing his treasure, his son. He'd only recently gotten his identity and his family back.

Guilt washed through him. At the encouragement of Daniel, who headed up the task force, this trip had been his idea. A chance to get out and do something fun with Raina and his sons and maybe talk about the future. Things in his home had been awkward since his return. Raina had assumed the role of parent in his absence. After he'd been presumed dead, she'd moved into his house to give the boys a sense of continuity. And he had asked her to stay for the same reason. All of that was a short-term plan.

Now all those plans had been blown to pieces once again. What if he was facing yet another tragedy?

He stared at the long stretch of road before him praying for the safety of his son.

TWO

After she made the call to Daniel, Raina handed Kenyon back his phone.

As she gazed through the windshield, a tightness snaked around her chest. They'd gone a mile without seeing any sign of the dark sedan. She lifted her head, trying to see above the huge truck in front of them. The car farther up the road was the right color, but she couldn't tell much else at this distance.

Austin spoke from the back seat. "Hey, that's our campground."

"Yes," said Raina.

"I saw that car. The one Beacon went for a ride in."

Raina jerked in her seat then stared back at Austin. "In the campground?"

Austin still held his juice box. He nodded.

"Are you sure?" Kenyon's voice filled with intensity.

"Yes," said Austin.

Raina gazed at him as if to ask an unspoken question. Did they trust the observations of a child? Kenyon slowed down and pulled off the road.

"Raina, you want to know what Austin's nickname has been ever since he could talk?" Kenyon must've picked up on what her expression had implied.

Raina shook her head. She was grateful Kenyon had

gotten his memory back. She now realized there was a whole history he'd shared with his sons and with his wife when she was alive that she had only been a cursory part of. "What was his nickname?"

Austin spoke from the back seat, kicking his legs. "Old Eagle Eyes."

Kenyon turned the car around and headed back toward the campground. He handed Raina his phone again. "Let the others know where we've gone."

Raina made the call to Daniel and informed him they'd turned into the camp. "Can you let Deputy Kelcey know?" Zach and Daniel were in separate cars.

"Sure, we're actually not to that turnoff yet," said Daniel. "Both of us were headed toward the park."

Kenyon turned into the camp. "Okay, buddy, where did you see the car?"

Austin sat up higher in his seat and lifted his head. "There."

Peanut looked out the window as well.

He pointed at a parking lot beside a small store, where people could rent bicycles or get supplies they'd forgotten. There was no dark sedan with a mismatched door parked there.

She fought off the doubt and despair that danced around the edges of her emotions. "I'll run inside and talk to the clerk."

"Great," said Kenyon. "Can you take Austin? Peanut and I can start searching the camp. I'll leave Chewy at the cabin. Peanut will be able to help track. Zack's K-9, Amber, will for sure be a help. We can use Beacon's jacket that he left in the back seat to get a scent off of." He glanced at his K-9. "Don't know what I'd do without my partner."

During Kenyon's absence, Peanut had been with another Plains City detective, West Cole, who was also on the DGTF. West had recently married Raina's sister, Trish.

A hundred what-ifs bombarded Raina as she unbuckled, got out of the car and pulled Austin from his car seat. What if the woman was here to buy something and had left the campground? What if Austin had been mistaken?

She entered the store, which had a low ceiling. Not much light came through two small windows. The clerk was a teenage girl with long braids and braces who barely looked up from her phone when Raina came in. "Can I help you?"

"I'm wondering if a woman came in here with a little boy just a few minutes ago." She pointed at Austin. "The little boy would look like his twin."

"'Cept I have a owie on my finger," said Austin. "And Beacon doesn't know his shapes."

The teenager shook her head. "I had three customers in the last twenty minutes. An older man and two women who came in separately. No kids."

She probably hadn't noticed much if she was on her phone like she was now.

I have to try.

"Did you notice a dark sedan in the parking lot? It has a back door that is a different color."

"I kind of focus on what is going on inside the store," said the clerk.

Raina's hope began to sink as she headed toward the door. They had used up precious time. If Austin had been mistaken and the woman had gone into Hot Springs, it would be that much harder for anyone to find her and Beacon. "Okay, thank you."

The teen lifted her gaze from the phone. "This seems really important to you."

"His brother is missing." Her voice faltered as tears rimmed her eyes.

The girl pushed the phone to the side. "Oh, wow. I'm sorry. I didn't realize."

Her throat had gone so tight she couldn't speak. Raina

managed a nod and headed toward the door. The bell dinged as she stepped outside into the crisp autumn air. Her heart was so weighted by fear, it physically hurt. Kenyon hadn't called yet with any kind of news. She could walk from here to the cabin they'd rented. She felt a numbness settle in around her as she took the first step on the well-trod dirt. Their search in the campground might be in vain.

She heard the bell again, and the clerk came outside. "Hey, I just remembered something."

Raina turned to face the girl, who tugged on one of her braids. "Yes."

"I don't know if it's important or not," said the store clerk.

Raina didn't want to let herself become hopeful. "Please tell me."

"One of the women bought one of our Wind Cave coloring books and some crayons. I just thought of that. Kind of weird she would get something like that if she didn't have a kid unless it was a gift for someone." The girl shrugged. "I don't know if it means anything."

Raina's spirits lifted as she reached out toward the girl and squeezed her hand. "Thank you. That's very helpful." Maybe they were on the right track, thanks to Old Eagle Eyes.

The teen shrugged. "I hope you find the kid." She wandered back toward the store with her hands in her pockets.

Just as she was about to run to the rented cabin, Zach Kelcey pulled into the parking lot. She knew many of the officers because her sister Trish was a Plains City officer. Still holding Austin, Raina hurried over to Zach as he got out of his patrol vehicle. He was a tall, muscular man.

"Kenyon called me," he said. "He's already searching the campground with Peanut. We're here to help. Daniel's headed toward Hot Springs just in case we're wrong." He pointed to the back seat, where his K-9, Amber, a black Lab, was in her kennel. "He said he'd leave the jacket behind at the cabin for Amber to get a scent off of."

"Our cabin is just around the corner and up the road a piece, number five."

"Hop in. I'll take you there."

She hurried around the vehicle and jumped into the front passenger seat, holding Austin. "Kenyon said your dog has found lots of missing children."

Zach's dark eyes grew serious, and he combed his fingers through his tousled brown hair. "Amber's got a reputation for that, yes."

They arrived at the cabin a minute later. Raina flung open her door. Zach got out and deployed Amber.

Just this morning they'd checked into the cabin and left their suitcases and supplies to tour Wind Cave.

That seemed like a lifetime ago. Life could change in an instant. Kenyon had left the blue jacket on the steps. She grabbed it and handed it to Zach, who placed it in front of Amber's nose. She sat Austin down on the step and went inside to get the double stroller where Chewy was resting on his bed. Raina had adopted Chewy as a puppy for the boys after Peanut had been reassigned. Chewy lifted his head while his tail thumped on the cushion.

"You watch the place, buddy."

When she came back outside, Amber was circling around the area. Zach followed, holding the leash.

"Did Beacon play outside at all before you headed off to the cave?"

"Yes, the boys ran around a bit when we got here."

"She might be picking up on an old scent." Zach still held the light blue jacket. The dog tugged on the lead. "She's got something." Zach smiled and waved at her as the dog picked up speed.

"I'll start asking people in the campground if they've

seen anything." Raina crossed her arms over her body and studied the other cabins while Austin crawled into the stroller. She didn't see Kenyon or Peanut anywhere. The campground was large, stretching way back toward the river. Their cabin was closer to the road.

Families sat at the picnic tables outside. Hadn't that been their plan, to have lunch at the park after taking the tour? She looked down at Austin as he sat in his stroller. "You're probably starving by now, huh?"

Austin nodded his head and touched his tummy.

She hurried back into the cabin and grabbed the snack bags she'd put together from the box of food she'd brought with her.

She headed toward the door but turned and picked up a second snack package. Beacon would be hungry too when they found him. She wasn't going to give up hope.

Kenyon jogged behind Peanut as the dog kept her nose to the ground. The beagle was so intent on her task it was hard to keep slack on the long lead. Peanut's primary training was in weapons detection, but most K-9s could track a strong scent. As Kenyon moved deeper into the campground, he could hear the sound of the rushing river. The trees that surrounded the cabins were thicker back here.

Before he got to their cabin to drop off Chewy, Kenyon had woven through the campground, not seeing the dark sedan anywhere. His detective mind speculated as to why this was happening. Was it connected to the trafficking case? Had the brothers who headed up the ring done this to get revenge on the unit for the sting last month? Even though they had yet to spot the sedan, he'd trust Peanut's nose over his own observations.

When he looked over his shoulder, he saw Zach headed toward him, with Raina not far behind pushing Austin in the stroller. Raina had stopped to talk to some kids who were playing outside their cabin, probably finding out if they'd seen anything.

She would know to hang back with Austin. If they did find Beacon with his kidnapper, the situation could get dangerous. He had no idea if the woman was armed or not. When he put Chewy in the cabin, he'd grabbed his personal firearm and brought it with him. Zach drew a little closer. Amber had picked up on the same scent as Peanut.

Peanut pulled hard on the lead then sat down outside a cabin that appeared unoccupied. There was no car parked outside. The curtains were drawn. When he tried the door, it was locked.

Kenyon bent toward the beagle. "Are you sure?"

Peanut remained in a sit position with her nose in the air. Zach and Amber arrived at the cabin. Amber sat down as well.

"Looks like the dogs think this is the one. Door is locked."

"Those windows look like they slide open," said Zach. "The dogs alerting gives us probable cause to enter."

"I'll go in. You cover me." Kenyon stepped forward and maneuvered the window open. Zach drew his weapon and pressed close to the wall of the cabin. Amber sat on her haunches, keeping her eyes on her partner.

Kenyon pulled back the curtain enough to see the living room. No sign anyone was there. Maybe they were wrong about this. He scanned the whole area. Then he saw a single duffel bag on the far side of the living room/kitchen partially hidden by a sofa. Someone was staying here.

"I'm going in," said Kenyon.

After pulling his gun, he put his leg through the window and crawled in. Once his feet touched the wood of the floor, he stepped toward the door and unlocked it. Zach came inside with his police-issue gun drawn. The cabin was quiet.

Except for the overnight bag by the sofa, there was no indication anyone had been here.

Kenyon's feet creaked on the floorboards as he took a step toward one of the other rooms. This cabin had the same layout as the one he and Raina had rented. A big open room with living room and kitchen, and two bedrooms on the far side of the cabin with a shared bathroom in the middle.

The doors to both bedrooms were closed. Kenyon signaled to Zach to clear one bedroom while he moved toward the other. As he drew closer, he heard the faintest tapping coming from within the room.

Zach reached to open the door of the other room and stepped in. Kenyon took in a breath and pushed the bedroom door open. Joy burst through him at what he saw.

Beacon sat at a kid-size table with his back to the door. A coloring book and crayons were laid out on the table. Beacon swirled the green crayon across the page.

Kenyon had time to holster his weapon before Beacon turned. The sense of elation he felt made him feel like he could fly.

The boy smiled. "Daddy."

Kenyon was so relieved, so ecstatic, that it caused pain in his chest. His muscles had turned to mush. He collapsed to his knees and held his arms wide open. "Hey, little buddy."

Beacon scooted his chair back and ran toward his dad. Kenyon wrapped his arms around his son. If only he could freeze this moment in time when his son was safe in his arms. "I was so worried about you." He leaned his head back to look into his son's blue eyes, resting a hand on his cheek. "Are you okay?"

Beacon touched his soft fingers to Kenyon's face where his eyes had glazed. "I'm sorry, Daddy. The lady said I should go with her. She said you wanted me to do that."

Zach lingered outside the door. "Hey, Beacon."

Kenyon had a hundred questions to ask Beacon but none of that mattered right now. He'd put on his police hat later. Right now, he just wanted to be Daddy. "She didn't hurt you at all, did she?"

Beacon shook his head. "She said to stay here and color. She's going to get me apple juice and chicken nuggets."

That meant the woman would probably be coming back.

Kenyon hugged his son again while Zach headed toward the door. "I'll let Raina know the good news."

Kenyon rose to his feet, still holding his son close. "I'm just glad you're safe and here with me."

He didn't want to stop holding Beacon, didn't want the moment to end. He kissed the top of his son's head and held him tight as he walked across the living room floor.

"Was that lady bad, Daddy?" Beacon's soft fingers touched Kenyon's cheek.

Beacon appeared unharmed and not frightened. "I don't know what's going on with her."

Maybe the kidnapping had nothing to do with the trafficking case. Maybe someone he had previously arrested wanted revenge on him now that he was back on the job.

A minute later, Raina and Austin were at the door with Zach behind them.

Austin raised his hands in the air. "Beacon."

Beacon wiggled from his father's embrace. Kenyon put him on the floor so he could run to give Austin a hug.

Raina stepped toward him, kneeling with open arms. Color had come back into her cheeks. She'd looked so pale before. She took both the boys into a hug. "We're so glad you're okay, Beacon."

"I was scared for you," said Austin. "That lady took you away."

Tears flowed down Raina's face.

Kenyon watched the three of them together.

She really loves my sons.

Things were so uncertain right now. Raina thought she would be raising the twins as a single mom. It was clear that their attachment to her was strong. He'd hoped that maybe this weekend away would give them a chance to talk about the future and her role in the twins' lives. His sons had suffered enough loss with their mother dying and thinking their father had died too... Though, Beacon had believed all along that Kenyon was alive. He'd claimed to have seen him one night through his bedroom window. Kenyon's brain had been foggy back then. For the nine months when his memory had been so fractured, only vague images of his old life had floated through his mind. Pictures that he wasn't sure what they meant. In working with the memory recovery expert, he realized he had at one point returned to his house where Raina was living with the boys without consciously understanding why he'd been drawn there.

Images of a beautiful redheaded woman had flashed through his mind as well. The image of her lovely face had given him comfort in the months when he was unsure of who he was. He now understood that the woman who skirted around the edges of his damaged memory had been Raina.

And that realization had changed everything. He was attracted to his best friend. The months he'd spent with her since returning home had only made that attraction harder to shake. He needed space from her to preserve the relationship they had, but he needed to be able to parent as well. If she moved out, how would that affect Beacon and Austin? He and Raina had been friends for a long time, and he didn't want to lose that either.

With her arms still wrapped around the boys, Raina gazed up at him.

Zach had opened the duffel and was rummaging through

it. "Just clothes in here. No indication of who this belongs to." His radio crackled and Daniel's voice came across the line.

"I just spotted the dark sedan with a woman driving outside Hot Springs. Looks like she turned to head back your way. I lost her in traffic on the highway though."

"How far away are you from the campground?"

"About ten minutes out," said Daniel.

"We'll be ready for her," said Zach. "We have to assume she's headed back this way." Zach let off the talk button.

Kenyon moved toward Raina and the boys. "Zach, why don't you and Amber watch the entrance of the campground? I need to get Raina and the boys back safe in our cabin, then I'll head back here."

Raina had already lifted Austin up and was headed toward the door.

"Carry me, Daddy," said Beacon.

Kenyon lifted Beacon up.

The boy wrapped his arms around Kenyon's neck. Kenyon kissed Beacon's forehead, thanking God that his son was safe.

By the time he stepped outside, Raina was strapping Austin into the double stroller. He put Beacon in the empty seat, resting his hand on Raina's back.

"I'll walk most of the way with you. I need to get back here as fast as I can." He didn't want to put Beacon in danger again though if the kidnapper should see him out in the open when she drove through the campground.

Raina turned toward him when he rested his hand on her back, her green eyes shining. "I hope you catch her."

"Me too." He didn't want to think about the possibility of the woman being at large and having the opportunity to come for his son again.

THREE

When Kenyon took over pushing the stroller, Raina was concerned that the pace at which they were moving would frighten the boys. He was jogging on the gravel road. The boys bounced in their seats.

Her gaze traveled across the camp, scanning the side roads and the areas around the other cabins as they ran.

"Daddy, why are we going so fast?" Austin's voice jiggled as he spoke.

Kenyon slowed a little, glancing nervously at Raina.

"We just need to get to the cabin, honey." She reached out to touch Austin's head.

The back of their cabin came into view. Kenyon stopped and stepped aside. "I'll let you take over with the boys." He reached out and touched his hand to her cheek. "You'll be all right?"

She nodded. Kenyon took off running toward the cabin by the river. He'd commanded Peanut to stay at the cabin. As she pushed the stroller the short distance to their cabin, the warmth of Kenyon's touch lingered. She parked the stroller outside and helped both boys get unstrapped.

She pulled the snack she'd grabbed earlier from her coat pocket and gave it to Beacon. "I bet you're hungry."

Beacon took the package.

"Can we eat outside?" Austin angled his body toward the picnic table.

"No." The word came out with a little too much intensity.

Austin blinked several times, a response she knew revealed his nervousness.

Though fear coiled around her like a snake, she didn't want to transmit that to the boys.

She softened her voice. "Let's just go inside, guys." The last thing she wanted to do was scare them, but the danger was real. That woman who had taken Beacon was most likely headed back to the camp.

She ushered the boys inside and locked the door behind her. "Why don't you two sit at the table? I'll get you some juice to go with your snack."

Austin took a seat, but Beacon ran toward her and wrapped his arms around her legs.

Her heart lurched. "Oh, sweetie." She kneeled down so she could take him into her arms.

"I don't want you to be afraid, Raina," said Beacon. While Austin tended to be the talker of the two boys, it was Beacon who often picked up on people's emotions.

Raina held him tight and rubbed his back. "Don't worry about me." Her throat went tight. "I'm just so glad you're okay, Beacon."

Austin had risen from his chair. He pointed at Beacon. "It was scary when you disappeared."

Beacon shook his head. "The lady didn't hurt me, but she kept calling me Joey." Beacon crossed his arms over his chest and scowled. "My name is Beacon. I told her that."

"It sure is." Raina made a mental note to tell Kenyon about the kidnapper insisting that Beacon was Joey. It might be important for figuring out what the motive for her taking Beacon had been. "Now both of you go sit at the table. I'll get you something to drink."

Raina retrieved juice boxes from the food supply she'd brought with her and helped the boys open their snack bag, which contained crackers and slices of cheese. She sat down as well.

"Are you hungry?" Beacon shoved a cracker in his mouth.

She hadn't eaten since breakfast when they'd left Plains City. Her stomach was so tied up in knots, she didn't think food was such a good idea.

"When is Daddy getting back?" Austin took a sip of his juice. "He said we would go fishing."

"Soon I hope." She struggled to keep her voice even. As she watched them eat, she thought about how much the boys looked like their father. Same dark hair and blue eyes.

She'd know Kenyon since kindergarten, but they had become close friends when they both participated in 4-H. His uncle had a farm outside of town where they both boarded their prize animals. In their teen years, she and Kenyon had been part of a group that went mountain biking, something they still did together. Always something seemed to keep them together, but it was clear that Kenyon saw her as only friend material. Maybe he just couldn't get the picture out of his mind of her helping catch his prize pig and ending up covered in mud. Though she'd lost her tomboyish demeanor by high school, maybe Kenyon would always think of her that way.

When her parents died when she was nineteen, it was Kenyon who saw her through such a hard time. That was when she had felt her heart open up to him, wishing that they could be more than friends. At first, she thought the attraction was driven by grief and needing someone strong to cling to, but the feelings had not faded as the years went by. Once Kenyon met his wife in college, she'd let go of that dream, choosing to be happy for him and backing away from the friendship for the sake of Kenyon's marriage.

Raina gazed at the two little boys and let out a heavy breath. The truth was she'd loved Kenyon for a long time, even if he didn't reciprocate.

Austin made his Goldfish cracker move up and down as though it were swimming through the water. "Hope Daddy finds that lady so we can go fishing."

Raina rose from her chair and moved toward the window. Outside, children played and adults sat in lawn chairs. A peaceful contrast to what Kenyon, Zach and Daniel might be facing just a short distance away.

She prayed for their safety. She didn't know what she'd do if she lost Kenyon a second time.

Once he knew that Raina and the boys would be safe inside where they couldn't be seen, Kenyon had sprinted back to the cabin where he'd found Beacon, Peanut waited for him by the cabin door. If the woman had returned in his absence, Peanut would have sounded the alarm.

He and Peanut stepped inside the cabin and peered out. He pulled his phone out and called Zach.

"Anything?"

"No, she should have been here by now. Daniel radioed that he's almost to the campground."

Kenyon stared out the front window. "Strange."

"I'll let you know if that status changes," said Zach.

"Do you think there's another way to get into the camp?"

"If there is, it doesn't show up on the map posted at the entrance," said Zach. "Once Daniel gets here, he'll watch the entrance and I'll search the camp, slowly working my way toward you. Maybe she did come in a different way."

"Or she got scared and didn't turn off." Kenyon gazed out the front window as he spoke. "She might have figured out she was being trailed or saw your patrol car."

"Could be."

"Stay in touch." Kenyon clicked the disconnect button as he moved through the house, glancing out each window until he was in the bedroom that looked out on the river. Peanut padded behind him. He scanned the area by the forest, seeing a sort of opening where the trees were far enough apart that there might be a dirt road there.

"Where is she Sweet Pea?"

Peanut thumped her tail and Kenyon leaned down to stroke her velvety ears.

"Don't know how I'd do my job without you." He drew his attention back to the window.

The dark sedan emerged through the trees. His heartbeat kicked up a notch. He stepped away from the window, hoping he hadn't been spotted.

Feeling the adrenaline course through his body, he pressed Zach's number. "She's here."

"Where at?"

"On a primitive road by the river," said Kenyon.

"I'm less than a minute away from you," Zach responded.

He moved to the living room. Keeping his body out of view, he tilted his head so he could see the car coming toward the cabin. The woman got out as if to move toward the door, but then looked around nervously.

Crouching, Kenyon pulled his gun and headed toward the door. Three rapid fire shots came through the window one of which almost hit Peanut. Adrenaline surged through him as he scrambled to get up against a wall and the beagle pressed him close to him.

He saw then that he'd left the window he crawled through open. That must have set off alarm bells for her.

He heard a car door slam and an engine roar to life. She was getting away.

With Peanut by his side, Kenyon burst out of the front door just in time to see the car disappear into the trees. Zach was coming toward him in his patrol vehicle. Kenyon ran toward him. After flinging open the passenger side door, he picked up Peanut and sat in the seat with her. There was no time to load her in the back.

Kenyon pointed to the opening in the trees. "She went back that way."

There was a reason the kidnapper had chosen a cabin at the back of the camp far away from the others—so she could come and go unnoticed. She must have known about the back road, which meant she was familiar with the camp.

Zach pressed the gas and zoomed toward the opening in the trees. The road was no more than a two-track.

Kenyon reached for the radio. "I'll let Daniel know. This road has to come out somewhere. Maybe he can catch her when she turns out on the highway."

The patrol car bounced on the rough road as Kenyon notified Daniel of what was going on.

Daniel responded, "I'll get out to the highway and see if I can find where that road comes out."

Kenyon signed off and placed the radio back in its slot.

The road narrowed even more as it curved through the thick forest. Branches scraped the side of the vehicle.

Kenyon peered ahead, not seeing the other car anywhere. The woman had less than a few minutes head start on them. She had to be here somewhere.

Zach increased his speed as he wove through the trees.

Daniel's voice came through the radio. "I've got a visual on her. She just pulled out on the highway. Headed toward Hot Springs."

They must be close to the highway too. Zach gunned the motor as the patrol car lumbered over the bumpy road. Peanut let out an excited yip.

Kenyon could see the highway up ahead.

Daniel's voice came through the radio. "I've lost sight of her. She had a good head start on me when I spotted her car."

Kenyon pulled the radio to his mouth. "We're right behind you."

He could see the highway up ahead.

Zach pulled out on the pavement, increasing his speed and turning the steering wheel into a curve. Within minutes, Daniel's patrol vehicle passed them going in the other direction.

"What's going on?" Zach tilted his head and let up on the gas.

Daniel voice came through the radio. "She pulled off the highway and turned around. I spotted the car but couldn't stop fast enough."

Zach pulled off on the next available shoulder and turned around to head back in the direction the other patrol car had gone.

Up ahead, the turn signal on Daniel's car blinked as he turned off on a gravel road. Zach followed him only a short distance down the road. He could see Daniel's car come to a stop by the parked sedan.

By the time they got to the dark sedan, Daniel had already deployed his K-9, a Great Dane named Dakota. Both men jumped out of the vehicle. Zach got Amber out of her kennel.

With Peanut beside him, Kenyon ran toward where Daniel stood by the sedan.

"The car is empty," said Daniel.

"Why would she run off like that?"

Daniel shrugged. "Maybe she has a hiding place around here with a gun stashed somewhere."

Kenyon did a quick scan of the area, seeing only fields, trees and a cabin that looked like it was about to fall down. If they were going to be shot at, it would have happened by now.

Kenyon moved toward the sedan. "Maybe the dogs can get her scent off something in the car."

He swung open the driver's side door. A fast-food bag with a grease stain sat on the passenger seat, along with a child's size football, new in the package, and a worn looking baseball cap. What had this woman had in mind? His heart squeezed tight. He thanked God Beacon was safe with Raina and Austin.

He grabbed the baseball hat, offering it first to Peanut and then handing it over to Daniel, who was standing close by. Peanut took off running up the dirt road. The other dogs followed. Peanut kept her nose to the ground, pulling hard on the lead as the other dogs caught up with her.

Peanut stopped then ran in circles trying to pick up the scent again. The other dogs responded in a similar way until Amber left the road but then circled back. They'd lost the scent.

Kenyon called Peanut to his side. He turned to look where the abandoned car was. They weren't that far from the highway. "Do you suppose she had another driver waiting here to pick her up?"

Zach shifted his weight as Amber sat at his feet. "Could be that's why the dogs lost the scent."

They could have passed the car on the highway and not realized it.

"If that's the case," said Daniel, "it means she has help."

That made her even more dangerous. "I need to get back to the cabin and check on Raina and the boys."

"Beacon will have to be questioned at some point," said Daniel.

"I know that. I'd like to keep it as informal as possible. I don't want my son to be afraid."

Daniel clamped his hand on Kenyon's shoulder. "I get that."

Daniel probably was understanding more and more what it meant to be a parent. Months ago, when Kenyon had still been missing and presumed dead, a little girl had been left outside the building shared by the ATF bureau and police headquarters with a note addressed to Daniel. The toddler, Joy, was the child of Daniel's half sister Serena. Up until Joy showed up in his life, Daniel hadn't known he had a half sister. His father had had an affair with a waitress that resulted in Serena being born. Daniel had recently learned that Serena was dying of cancer and staying in a hospice. Aside from Daniel's grandmother, he was Joy's only other relative. With the okay from child protective services, he'd been taking care of the little girl. Daniel had his grandmother take Joy to the hospice to see her mom often.

All three of the officers and their K-9 partners walked back toward the patrol cars.

Kenyon spoke up. "Raina and I will work on getting more information from Beacon. At some point we might need to do a police sketch. I prefer to do it at my home instead of bringing him into the police station so he's in a more relaxed environment."

They stopped at the abandoned sedan. The car looked really clean. Kenyon stared at the worn baseball hat, which he now saw was a child's size. Something about the sight of it seemed almost poignant.

"We need to gather that stuff for evidence. I've got bags in my vehicle." Zach walked toward his patrol car with Amber heeling beside him.

Kenyon opened the passenger door and checked the glove box for registration. Empty of course. Why else would the kidnapper abandon it so quickly?

Daniel turned to face Kenyon. "Sorry your vacation got ruined in the worst way. I gave you the time off hoping that it would give you and Raina a chance to regroup."

"I thought we might have some downtime to talk about the boys' future. Everything has been so hectic for the last month, so focused on me getting my memory back."

"Do you need more time?" said Daniel.

"I'll be back to work on Monday just as we planned." With the recovery of his memory, Kenyon had been reinstated as a detective with the Plains City PD and agreed to join the task force that had been formed in his absence.

"Only if you feel up to it," said Daniel.

People were still tiptoeing around him. Getting back to work would be the best thing for Kenyon. The explosion that had taken his memory and severed his life from all that mattered to him was connected to the gun trafficking investigation that had led to forming of the two-state task force. He wanted to catch the men who were moving guns around the Dakotas and ultimately seeking to sell them to gangs and other criminals in other states.

"Yeah, I feel up to it. I feel more than up to it," said Kenyon.

The truth was going back to work felt easier than trying to resolve where he and Raina stood with his sons. She'd stepped up in his absence and made huge sacrifices, even turning her house into a vacation rental and moving into his home so the kids would have stability. He didn't want to lose her friendship, but he needed to fully be a father to Beacon and Austin, to rebuild trust. Both of them needed to be wise about what they chose to do.

After Zach had gathered the evidence from the car and Daniel made a call to get the car towed and taken to the state crime lab, Kenyon loaded Peanut in the back seat of the patrol car and got in the passenger seat.

Zach dropped him off in front of the cabin where his vehicle was parked. When he stepped inside, Raina and the boys were seated around the coffee table working on a puzzle. She had thought to bring some things for indoor activities. Actually, Raina seemed to think of everything when it came to taking care of the twins.

She lifted her head, a question in her expression.

He shook his head and her features darkened. The woman who had taken Beacon for who knows what purpose was still out there. Would she come for him again? They wouldn't know until they had a name and could find a motive for the kidnapping.

One thing he knew for sure, they couldn't stay here any longer. If she was going to come for Beacon again, this would be the first place she'd look. The boys would be disappointed, but he wasn't about to take that kind of a chance with his sons' lives.

FOUR

Raina tried to focus on the recipe book she was looking through, but the noise of the twins playing in the next
room was distracting. The sword fight the boys were having
sounded a little brutal. Kenyon would step in if he needed
to. Both boys had been restless since they'd gotten home.
Cutting the weekend getaway short had been confusing
to them, even though Kenyon had promised to take them
fishing at the river that ran through town.

Once Kenyon had arrived at the cabin, they'd left immediately, stopping only to get Beacon checked out at an
urgent care and to grab a late lunch at a fast-food place.
They were home now…safe, but the boys had been stirred
up all day even after Raina fed them their favorite dinner,
mac and cheese.

She glanced up to see the rain pattering against the
kitchen window. No fishing today. Maybe tomorrow they
would be able to go fishing after church. Confinement was
not a good thing for three-year-old boys. Both she and Kenyon were working hard at presenting a calm and united
front, but the twins no doubt had picked up on the anxiety
they both battled over the kidnapping.

Kenyon sat in the living room recliner with the leg rest
up while he reread the reports on the gun trafficking in-

vestigation. Peanut and Chewy had settled into their dog beds close by.

Raina stared at the picture of an elaborate wedding cake. When she'd taken over as Beacon and Austin's parent, her job as a specialty baker had allowed her to be with them full-time while she worked from home. They often went with her when she made her deliveries to the coffee shops and cafés around town. She turned the page in the cookbook, hoping for inspiration. She had a wedding coming up, and she wanted to create something special for the bride and groom.

In the next room, Beacon cried out in pain. "Ouch, you hit me, Austin. That hurt."

Before she could even close the recipe book, Kenyon had jumped to his feet and rushed into the boys' room. She could hear him talking in a soothing but authoritative tone. The room grew quiet and Kenyon returned to the living room.

She looked up from where she was resting her elbows on the counter browsing the cookbook. "They're a little worked up, aren't they?"

"Yes, and they're taking it out on each other. I told them to take a break and do something separately."

She didn't have to peer into the room to know that Austin was playing with building blocks and talking to himself the whole time and Beacon was probably quietly flipping through a picture book. Though they were twins, their personalities were distinct. Austin was the extrovert, often speaking for the two of them, and Beacon was more introspective.

Kenyon moved toward her, standing on the opposite side of the kitchen island. Still resting her hands on the counter, she straightened her back and gazed into his blue eyes. "Yes?"

"We're going to need to talk to Beacon about what happened to him in order to figure out who that woman was and why she took him in the first place."

"What do you know so far?"

"This was planned out. The woman chose a cabin that was away from the others and had access to a road where no one would see her coming and going. My guess is she had been to that campground before and probably Wind Cave."

"So you think she went to Wind Cave looking to abduct a child."

"I just wonder if we were targeted because of something connected to my work. I'll spare you the details, but the guys involved in this trafficking case will stop at nothing to derail the investigation."

Raina shuddered. "It wasn't totally planned. She hadn't already bought the coloring book and she didn't have any food for him."

Kenyon nodded and rested his hand on the back of his neck, something he always did when he was thinking deeply.

Her throat went tight. Talking about what had happened made her nervous, but she needed to face this head-on if they were going to catch this woman. The outcome for today could have been so much worse. "Beacon mentioned that the woman kept calling him Joey."

"Interesting. There was a little boy's hat in the car she abandoned. Not a new one." Kenyon had explained earlier what had happened with the pursuit when the boys were out of earshot.

They both looked at each other for a long moment until Kenyon vocalized what she was thinking. "I wonder if she lost a child and Beacon looked like him. I'd have to check through my old case files to see if there was a child named Joey connected to any of my investigations."

"Do you think she might come for him again?" The tightness in her chest made it hard to get the words out.

"That's why we left the cabin. She doesn't know where we live."

"Yes, she does." A little voice came from the living room.

Beacon stood holding his picture book close to his chest. Raina wondered how much of the conversation he'd heard.

Kenyon rushed over to him and swept him up. He took the book and placed it on a nearby table. "You know we were talking about what happened to you today."

Beacon shoved his finger in his mouth and nodded.

Raina moved toward father and son. "Did you tell the lady where you lived?"

"I said my name was Beacon and I live in Plains City." He shook his head as his brow furrowed. "She wouldn't stop calling me Joey."

Fear pierced Raina's heart. So the kidnapper did know what city they lived in, and if she saw Beacon as some kind of substitute for a child she'd lost, she might come looking for him.

Kenyon stroked the back of Beacon's head. "I know that upset you."

The way Kenyon gazed at his son warmed Raina's heart. He'd come a long way in a short time in rebuilding connection.

She'd do anything to ensure that the boys had the best shot at a good life, even if it meant putting her own feelings and frustration about her future status on hold. What she and Kenyon needed to focus on was making sure the boys had stability from here on.

"Why don't you get Austin and we'll play a game together. Perfect thing to do on a rainy day," said Raina.

Beacon wiggled out of his father's grasp then gazed up at him. "Are you going to play?"

"I will. I have a phone call to make first."

Beacon hurried back into his bedroom.

Raina stopped. "What phone call?"

"I'm going to see if our tech analyst can figure out if any of my previous cases had a kid named Joey connected to them."

"She works on Saturday?"

"I don't think Cheyenne ever really stops working. Even if she'll officially engage with the case on Monday, I'm sure she'll start a database search even before that."

Knowing why the woman had targeted Beacon would probably be helpful. Kenyon grabbed his phone and moved toward his bedroom so the boys wouldn't hear the conversation. When he was on the threshold, he turned back to face her. "Raina, it wouldn't hurt when I'm at work for your sister to come over if she's off duty."

Raina's sister, Trisha, was a patrol officer with the Plains City PD. Kenyon was thinking that she and the boys might need some extra protection. "The kidnapper doesn't know your last name or exact address."

"We don't know anything for sure. Maybe being chased down by the police scared her off, but let's not take any chances," he added before stepping into the bedroom and closing the door.

The sound of the boys' laughter in the next room drifted toward Raina as she crossed her arms over her body and tried to push away the fear that danced around the corners of her mind. Kenyon hadn't set off any alarms, but he wasn't taking any chances either.

On Monday morning, Kenyon sat in his car staring at the four-story building that had been his place of work for years before the explosion that had taken his memory. He'd worked here first as a patrol officer before making detective. This place had once been so familiar to him—before it'd been wiped from his memory. He was a different man before the explosion. Much of the work he'd done to get his memory back was to return to the places that had been part of his life. He'd walked these halls and sat at his old desk with the specialist who was helping him.

There were still pieces missing from his growing up years. On Sunday, Raina had pulled out photo albums that she'd found to try to help him fill in the blanks, something they did together on a regular basis.

He reached over to pet Peanut, even as a tightness invaded his chest. Was he really ready to go back to work?

Yes, his inner voice answered.

Despite his doubts about returning to work, Kenyon had to go back. He wanted to catch the men responsible for wreaking havoc on his life and stop them from ruining more lives with their criminal deeds. The traffickers had set the explosion to keep evidence hidden from law enforcement, and Kenyon had suffered because of it. The twins had a birthday coming up, and he'd missed most of the past year with them. The traffickers had brought unbearable heartache to his boys…and to Raina.

He'd do everything he could to take the criminal ring down.

The reports he'd read had brought him up to speed on everything that had happened with the gun trafficking case in his absence. The operation was run by two brothers going under the aliases Hal and Brandon Jones. The brothers, whose criminal records had been revealed when the task force discovered their real last name was Murray, kept residences in both Fargo and Plains City.

Last month the team had gotten info that the brothers were escorting a gun shipment in North Dakota personally, so a sting had been set up in a vineyard to catch them in the act. Though the brothers had gotten away, the task force had confiscated four shipments of guns and caught some low-level players. One of those players, a driver named Alan Tate, had agreed to cooperate with the task force and gain intel for them. They learned that Hal was probably the brains behind the illegal endeavor and that Brandon could be volatile. The informant explained that he had witnessed Brandon kill an associate because he looked at him funny.

Kenyon took in a prayer-filled breath and let go of his trepidation before pushing open the door. It didn't matter if he was ready or not. He was a police officer, and he had a job to do.

By the time he had unloaded Peanut from his car, Daniel was standing at the door, holding it open for him.

"I saw you from my office window and thought I'd come down." The task force leader's warm smile helped him relax. Daniel, an ATF agent, had come all the way down from his office on the fourth floor to greet him. The DGTF couldn't have a better man to lead them. "Ready to hit the ground running?"

"Sure," said Kenyon.

"I'm sending you and West Cole out. Peanut's nose will come in handy. West's new K-9, a yellow Lab named Gus, is also trained in weapons detection. Our informant tells us that he heard of a shipment of guns being moved from close to Wind Cave to somewhere around Plains City. We weren't able to locate the guns by Wind Cave—just too much area to search. We're hoping to figure out where in Plains City they are bringing them to. They may already be somewhere in town. We know the brothers have used businesses and remote areas as hiding places in the past."

"Where do you think the guns might be hidden?"

"I'll answer that, but first, how is your son doing?" Daniel giving priority to the welfare of his son over what was going on with the case spoke volumes about who he was as a person.

"Medical exam didn't indicate he'd been harmed physically in any way." He tensed up when he spoke about what had happened to Beacon. "Kids are resilient, but I want to make sure he hasn't been affected emotionally. Raina's got Trisha helping her today. You know, just in case."

"I'm glad he's okay." They moved through the building toward the conference room where the task force met. "I'll give you the details about possible locations in the briefing."

They were outside of Cheyenne Chen's office. Swinging her chair around, Cheyenne turned her head away from the monitor to look at Kenyon. "Just the man I want to talk to."

Kenyon addressed Daniel. "Could I have a minute with her?"

"Sure," Daniel said. "The others should be arriving for the briefing in ten minutes or so."

Daniel headed up the hallway.

Kenyon stepped into Cheyenne's office. "I knew you'd find something out for me."

Cheyenne had pulled her long dark hair up in a bun. Her office had an abundance of plants along with two monitors, a laptop and a keyboard. "I did a search of your old cases."

"I don't remember a Joey being connected to any of my

cases, but you know how my memory is these days." He gave Cheyenne a friendly punch in the shoulder.

"That's why you have me," she said. "Do you remember a man named Devin Lane."

"Yeah, arrested for B and E of a house. I caught him in the act."

She nodded. "He's got out of prison recently. I did a search of newspaper articles against his name. An obituary came up. He was listed as the father of a four-year-old boy who drowned. The boy's name was Joey. The accident happened just before Devin's release."

"Sad. So maybe Devin thinks if he hadn't been jail… His son would still be alive. Maybe he blames me."

"You did say the woman had an accomplice. Maybe she's not the mastermind behind the kidnapping."

"Okay, so maybe we put a tail on Devin and see if anything turns up. Anything else?"

"I got to wondering why the kidnapping happened at the caves. So I worked that angle."

Cheyenne thought of everything when it came to an investigation. "You came up with something?"

"There was a three-year-old boy named Joey Starling who died from a fall in the cave, but it was ten years ago." She brought up an obituary with a photo of a dark-haired boy holding a baseball bat, a T-ball photo.

"So where is his mom at now?"

"That's just the thing. Mom and Dad both died last year. Joey's obituary says he was survived by a twelve-year-old sister, Tanya. Assuming she has kept her maiden name or never married, I should be able to track her down. I'll let you know when I do."

Kenyon cupped Cheyenne's shoulder. "Good work." He

took in a breath. "I got a briefing to get to." He headed down the hallway and up the stairs to the third floor.

Kenyon sat at the conference table with the other members of the task force who were currently in town. Not everyone was present. Many of the members lived in other towns in North and South Dakota and would only be brought in when needed. Zach Kelcey was still in town, though he lived close to Mount Rushmore. Jenna Morrow, a blue-eyed task force member with chestnut brown hair, was here from North Dakota, where she worked as a patrol officer in Fargo. She and her K-9 partner, Augie, had been key players in the sting that had taken place at the Red Valley Vineyard last month. West sat in a chair with Gus, a yellow Lab trained to detect firearms just like Peanut.

Daniel leaned forward and rested his hands on the conference table. "As you know, we have been tailing Hal and Brandon to become aware of the places they frequent around Plains City and learn where they might stash guns. Finding where those guns will be hidden is key. We need to catch the brothers in the act of transporting the guns. Today we're going to focus on searching possible locations."

Daniel listed the places they intended to search and made his assignments. "Kenyon and West, you head to the old amusement park outside of town."

"You mean Wild West Land?"

Daniel nodded. "Let's get this done."

Kenyon and West drove in separate vehicles to the location. Wild West Land had been a thriving business up until the time Kenyon was a teenager. They pulled up to an area surrounded by a tall chain-link fence. With the exception of a partly dismantled Ferris wheel and a merry-go-round for toddlers, most of the rides had been sold and hauled away. What remained were the dilapidated booths where the games had been played and the concessions had been sold. The Wild West theme was evident from the faded murals of cowboys in action on the sides of the buildings to the broken wagon with no wheels. Parts and pieces of rides were also scattered around.

Kenyon and Cole got out of their respective vehicles and deployed their K-9s. West walked over to Peanut and kneeled to pet her.

"How's my little Sweet Pea."

Peanut wagged her tail and licked his face. When Kenyon had been MIA, Peanut had been West's K-9.

West rose to his feet and reached out to shake Kenyon's hand and clamp the other hand on his shoulder. "Glad you're back on the job, man."

They had been friends from the time both of them had joined the force.

West turned his attention to Wild West Land. "When we tailed Hal, he stopped here. He parked his car and sat here for a long time."

Kenyon stared at the dilapidated amusement park. "Sad to see this place go to ruin. I know I came out here plenty of times when I was in high school."

West grinned before his expression turned serious. "Let's get to work," he said.

Though the fence was secured with a chain and lock, some of the chain link had been cut and bent back with holes large enough for a person to fit through. West and Gus slipped through, and Kenyon followed with Peanut. They walked past a weathered For Sale sign and a large plastic buffalo with chipping paint.

Piles of metal and other debris blocked much of their view of the place.

Kenyon gave Peanut the command to find guns. "Tools."

The dog put her nose to the ground and went to work. West moved in the opposite direction with his K-9. Peanut led him down the row of booths built to look like log cabins. The dog moved at a steady pace but never alerted.

Kenyon pressed the talk button on his radio while he kept walking. "Anything?" He'd grabbed the radio so he and West could communicate more easily.

"Not so far. Lot of garbage around the main concession building. Looks like someone may have been squatting here at some point."

Peanut continued to move forward as they came to the end of the booths.

Kenyon heard a noise.

"Stop." At his command, Peanut sat with her nose still in the air. A scraping noise that could be metal being rustled by the wind reached his ears. The sound he'd heard previously had been different.

He pressed the talk button on his shoulder radio. "Think I heard something over by the restrooms. Gonna check it out."

He moved around to the side of the last booth. The overcast sky indicated that rain was on the way. He and Peanut walked at a steady pace toward what had been the restrooms. Now the windows were broken, and one door hung by a single hinge while the other lay on the ground. A mural on the side of the concrete building depicted a wagon train moving through the hills of South Dakota.

A noise came from within the men's side of the restroom. Kenyon moved toward the dark threshold.

Rain sprinkled out of the sky.

Peanut barked three times. Something that was unusual for her.

What was making her nervous?

He peered into the dark interior of the restroom. He saw a broken toilet laying on its side and a door torn off one of the stalls. Peanut let out a low-level growl. After pulling his weapon, he took a step inside.

A flurry of dark rolling motion came toward him. Peanut barked several more times while she paced side to side and jumped up and down.

He pivoted in time to see a raccoon head for the shelter of a detached Ferris wheel chair turned upside down.

With his heart racing, Kenyon commanded Peanut to sit. The dog obeyed but didn't quite rest her back legs on the ground. "I know you'd like to get that guy, but that's not our job."

West's voice came through the radio. "Everything all right there? That was quite a ruckus."

Kenyon turned his head to speak into his radio. "False alarm." As he released the talk button and lifted his head, he caught a flash of motion in his peripheral vision. Separated from the rest of the park was an area where customers formerly could take horseback rides. Now the area consisted of empty barns and a corral that was falling down. Something had moved within one of the three barns. It could be another animal or some detached part of the building being blown by the wind.

He could see West and the yellow Lab on the other side of the park as they headed toward what used to be a concrete parking lot, now broken up and filled with debris.

He drew his attention back to the corrals. "I'm going to check out the old horse riding arena."

"Got it. We're moving in toward where the offices used to be."

Holstering his gun, Kenyon jogged toward the barns with Peanut keeping pace. His attention focused on the area outside the chain-link fence. The place was overgrown with brush and trees, but as he drew closer, he saw the distinct outline of a vehicle. The vehicle, which could be a van or maybe an SUV, was almost the same colors as the trees and brush and partially hidden by them.

He spoke in a low voice. "Suspicious vehicle just outside the fence by the corrals. I need to investigate the interior of the barns. Saw something move in there."

"Headed toward my car to go check the vehicle out." West's voice was jumpy, indicating that he was running as he spoke into his radio.

Kenyon slowed as he approached the barn where he thought he'd seen movement. The large doors were missing, allowing him to see inside. As he drew closer, he could discern a life-size teacup that had been part of a ride as well as several horse stalls.

Rain pattered on his head.

He stepped toward the open area. A weight hit him from the side, knocking him to the ground. The man was on top of him, pummeling his head and chest.

Kenyon twisted his body away from the assault, seeking to get to his feet while he reached for his gun. The attacker dove at him again while he was on his knees. Kenyon landed several blows to the man's face. He was muscular and well over six feet tall.

Peanut circled the wrestling match and barked. The tall man landed a blow to Kenyon's chest and stomach that stunned him for a moment and made him stumble backward.

The man turned to run toward where the vehicle was. The rain turned to a downpour as Kenyon recovered from the assault and pursued the suspect across the muddy field.

Kenyon sprinted, closing the distance between the two

of them. When he was only feet from tackling the culprit, he yelled, "Police, stop."

The man swooped down to pick something up off the ground and then turned to face Kenyon with a metal bar in his hand. Kenyon moved to draw his gun but was hit in the shoulder before he could. Pain radiated through his gun arm. The man came at his head again. Kenyon dodged that blow by twisting away, which exposed his back. The man hit him twice. Kenyon doubled over.

The move left him stunned for only a few seconds. When he looked up, the man had made it to the fence and was crawling through the opening. Kenyon caught a glimpse of West's patrol vehicle on the far side of the fence.

With Peanut close behind, he slipped through the opening in the fence and pushed through the brush to where the vehicle was. As he approached, he could hear the engine in what he now saw was a gray van start up, and it sped away. He pulled his gun, taking note of the first two numbers of the license plate before it got too far away to read it. He fired but couldn't get an accurate shot at this distance.

West pulled up beside him with the engine still running. In one swift motion, Kenyon picked up Peanut and jumped into the passenger seat.

Before Kenyon had even closed the door, West pressed the accelerator and headed toward what looked like a dirt road. The back of the van came into view within a few minutes as it turned onto a paved road.

The driver headed toward a suburb that contained many three-story apartment buildings. West turned where the van had gone, but when they got on the street, the van was not visible.

"Where did he go?"

He slowed down while Kenyon scanned the side streets

as they rolled past. The apartment buildings blocked much of their view.

West drove through the neighborhood and then backtracked to where they had entered the suburb. They still didn't see the van anywhere. He could have slipped down one of the alleys and hidden.

"Wonder if he had anything to do the gun smuggler case."

"He sure ran like a guilty man, and he attacked me. Peanut never alerted to the scent of any guns though," said Kenyon.

"Neither did Gus. The guy could have been scouting locations for possible hiding places."

"Or he could be completely disconnected from the case." Kenyon shifted in his seat. "He's easy enough to identify. He was a big guy with distinctive features, and I got the first two numbers off the gray van."

"Shouldn't be hard to track him down," said West.

"I'll phone Cheyenne." Kenyon dialed her number and gave her the info on the van, license number and a description of the driver.

"I'll get right on it. We have someone watching Devin Lane." Her voice dropped half an octave. "I have some more info on Joey's sister. I'll send it to you. The juvenile records are sealed, so all the info is for after she turned eighteen."

Her comment sounded a bit mysterious, and he picked up on her dark tone. Like maybe she had come across something, but it wasn't conclusive enough to share.

"Do you have a last known address?"

"Yes, she lives in River's End, ten miles from Plains City. I'll send that to you along with the other stuff."

West arrived at the front of Wild West Land where Kenyon had left his vehicle. He and Peanut got out.

West stuck his head out the window. "See you back at headquarters." He rolled up his window and drove away.

After loading Peanut in the back seat, Kenyon sat behind the wheel and opened up the text Cheyenne had sent him while rain pattered on the window. The first thing he saw was a newspaper photo of a teenage Tanya standing outside Wind Cave with people identified as her parents. All three of them held candles. The caption said the family had returned to hold a vigil for Joey as they did every year. The next picture was a driver's license photo of an adult Tanya. Kenyon kept scrolling through a series of documents. What he read next made him feel like he'd been punched in the gut.

Tanya had been dishonorably discharged from the army for emotional instability. He kept reading. Her training was in weapons and explosives.

Even as he sat still and took in a deep breath, he could feel the adrenaline course through his body. He needed to make sure his sons were okay.

He called Raina's number, but it went to voicemail. Not good. Then he tried Trisha's phone.

"Hello?"

The sound of children shouting and laughing in the background was like a balm to his soul.

"Trisha, everything all right there?"

"We're just fine and dandy. The boys are playing nice with Gabriel and Chewy." Gabriel was Trish's one-year-old boy. He'd been born shortly before Kenyon's accident, and Raina doted on him.

"What about Raina? She didn't answer her phone when I called."

"She might have been driving and not able to answer.

She's out doing her deliveries. Because of everything that has been going on, she's kind of behind on her work."

The news that the boys were safe should have helped him relax. "But you haven't heard from Raina?"

"She doesn't check in every ten minutes. What's going on anyway? How would the kidnapper even find you guys?"

"I just don't want to take any chances."

"I understand. We've taken precautions. The kids are only playing inside."

"Thank you. How long ago did Raina leave?"

"Less than ten minutes ago," said Trish.

"Okay. Thanks for watching the boys. Talk to you soon." He hung up and tried Raina's number again. Still no answer. He had to know that she was safe too. He wanted to hear her voice. Kenyon pulled away from the ruins of the amusement park and headed back toward town with Raina still on his mind.

He'd try her again in a minute while he drove back to headquarters. By the time he got there, Cheyenne might have tracked down who owned the van so they could figure out if he had any connection to the trafficking ring. What he really wanted to do was question the two suspects who may have taken Beacon. But that would have to wait.

FIVE

The rain was coming down hard and fast by the time Raina pulled into the parking lot to make her first delivery. The shop that served tea was one of her long-time customers.

After pulling the hood of her raincoat over her head, she pushed open the door and ran to the back of her SUV, opening the hatch. The tea cakes and lemon bars were in spill proof containers with lids.

The bell rang as she stepped inside, and the owner, a man named Clive, emerged from the back of the shop. He was a balding man with a paunch who always wore a suit. There were only a few customers inside. All three people sat alone watching the rain or writing in journals while they sipped their tea.

Clive held up his hands. "Raina, my favorite person." His British accent was still evident though he'd lived in the states for years.

She threw back the hood of her raincoat. "And why is that?"

"You came just in time. I sold the last lemon bar to a woman who commented on your ad and wanted to buy more." Clive pointed to the eight by ten sheet of paper in a plastic holder that featured a picture of her holding a plate of her baked goods. A slot with her business cards was attached to the ad.

"Oh, maybe I'll get a specialty order out of the deal," said Raina as she handed Clive the tray of goodies over the display counter.

"Don't know about that. The woman said she was from out of town."

"Oh, well, glad to hear she liked them." She turned toward the door. "Would love to chat but got to make a bunch more stops."

As she hurried back outside, she could hear her phone ringing in her coat pocket. By the time she'd opened the door of her car and got in, the phone had rung three times. She pulled it out.

Kenyon. And it looked like the previous call that had come while she was driving was from him too. She pressed the connect button. He'd called twice in a short span of time. Her first thought was that something had happened with the twins.

"Kenyon. Is everything all right?"

"Glad to hear your voice." His words fused with warmth.

The emotion behind his words surprised her. "Glad to hear yours too, Kenyon." Though he had always been a good listener when she needed to work through something, he was never one to call just to chat. "What's going on?"

"I was concerned about you when you didn't answer your phone."

His worry about her was touching. "Trisha is watching the twins so I thought I would make some deliveries."

"I know that. I called Trisha when you didn't answer." There was a short pause. When he spoke again his tone had grown darker. "Cheyenne dug up some information about two possible suspects behind Beacon's. One is a man, Devin Lane, who I arrested. His son Joey drowned while he was incarcerated. The other, Tanya Starling, had three-year-old brother named Joey who fell to his death in the cave ten years ago."

"How tragic."

"I've got a copy of a driver's license photo that we can show Beacon to confirm if she's the woman who took him. That would help us rule out Devin."

"I hope that won't upset Beacon," she said.

"I was thinking the same thing, but if we're going to catch this woman, it has to be done."

"I just wish it hadn't happened. I worry about how it's going to affect Beacon down the line, even though it doesn't seem like she harmed him in any way," said Raina.

He cleared his throat. The low-level hum of an engine indicated that he was driving. "Both suspects have concerning histories. Devin's son's death is more recent."

Raina put the phone on speaker and set it on the console so she could start her car. The windshield wipers worked furiously, creating an intense rhythm. "What did you find out?"

"Devin was put away for burglary, but he also had a history of assault. Tanya doesn't have a criminal history, but there is the suggestion of instability, and she has military training in weapons and explosives."

The news made her feel a little lightheaded as she pulled out of the parking lot onto the street. Both suspects sounded unstable. The other cars were murky images with smeared headlights. She drove for several minutes before saying anything. "That means both of them could be dangerous." If they hadn't found Beacon when they did, what might have happened to him? She couldn't let her mind go there.

"Potentially, yes. The only info Cheyenne had access to happened after Tanya turned eighteen. She's going to dig to see if she can find out more."

"So she has a juvenile record that was sealed?" Raina

turned onto a road that led out of town to a bed and breakfast she needed to drop off muffins and two chocolate silk tortes to. The road was bordered by forest on one side and fields on the other. "I'm sure the boys are all right, but I'll get back there as fast as I can. I'm headed to the B and B the Bensons own, and then I have two more deliveries to make on the other side of town." The Bensons were an older couple who went to her church and had been long time customers.

"I've got to file a report and take Peanut to search another location. I'll get home as fast as I can."

"Sounds good." She was about to say good-bye when she checked the rearview mirror. Fear spread through her. A car was zooming toward her. What was going on? Her heart pounded as she pressed the gas. The other car closed the distance between them. She gripped the steering wheel as metal crunched against metal and her car lurched forward. She dropped the phone gripping the wheel with both hands.

She screamed and the phone slid across the console onto the floor. She was hit again from behind before she had recovered from the first collision.

Raina pressed the gas, trying to get away.

The car got even with her, and Raina felt a burst of fear as it swung closer. She couldn't see the driver, but the vehicle rammed into her from the side, once…twice. The steering wheel jerked in her hands as she tried to get control of the vehicle. She rolled off the road into a field and down into a steep ditch. The impact made her whole body shake and her jaw clenched. The other car remained on the road. Two people dressed in rain ponchos got out.

She shifted into reverse, but when she pressed the gas the wheels spun. The car was stuck in the mud. The two people moved closer toward her. Raina pushed open the door and jumped out, headed toward the shelter of the trees.

She ran flat-out. The Bensons' B and B had to be over a quarter mile away still. When she peered over her shoulder, she caught glimpses of two people in dark rain ponchos moving steadily toward her.

A gunshot echoed around her, causing her to freeze momentarily before she dove deeper into the forest. Her heart pounded as she kept running, trying to orient herself to get back to the road so she could find her way to the Bensons' place.

When she peered over her shoulder, she saw only one of the figures. She scanned the area. Where had the other one gone? The trees thinned, allowing her to see the road up ahead. When she glanced behind, her wrecked car came into view along with the car that had run her off the road.

Raina gasped for breath as she remained in the shelter of the trees but with a view of the road. One of the figures ran back to the car and started it up. She gasped. The culprit would run her down if she tried to get back on the road. How was she going to get to safety?

Though she could not see the other person who had followed her into the trees, she had to assume she was still being pursued on foot as well. Weaving through the trees, she kept running in the general direction of the B and B but staying away from the road.

Then she heard it. The faint sound of sirens in the distance. She had not had time to hang up from her call with Kenyon. He must have heard her scream.

Another gunshot reverberated around her. Her heart lurched. She willed herself to go faster.

Keep running. Help is on the way.

She was so deep in the trees she could no longer see the road. The sirens had grown even louder.

Her leg muscles were aching from fatigue. Gasping for

air, she slowed down, looking for signs of the pursuer. She saw only the trees that surrounded her and blocked her view of the road.

The sirens had stopped.

Though it was hard to discern through the downpour, she thought she heard her name being called. Kenyon? She ran toward the sound until she was at the edge of the forest. Kenyon with Peanut paced a short distance from the road, calling for her.

"I'm here." Her voice sounded weak. She took in a breath and shouted, "Kenyon, over here!"

He came toward her. She ran through the trees and fell into his arms.

"It's all right," he said. "I've got you."

Feeling like his own heart would burst, Kenyon held Raina. The sound of her screaming in terror over the phone had been like a knife through him. The high-speed drive to get to her before something bad happened had caused images of what his life would be like without her. She was crying and trying to talk at the same time. He made a shushing noise and ran his hand over her long red hair.

"You don't need to talk right now," he said.

He was glad he'd called for backup while he was racing across town praying that he wouldn't be too late.

A Plains City police officer in a patrol car had been able to pursue the fleeing car so he could look for Raina. The sight of her stuck vehicle had struck a chord of fear inside him.

She pulled away from him and gazed into his eyes. One thing he had always admired about her was how level-headed she was. In their growing up together, he'd witnessed her be unfazed by wrecks on mountain bikes and being chased by bulls.

As he looked into her green eyes, he could see that she was truly rattled by what had happened to her. Peanut pressed close to her legs and offered a sympathetic whine.

He stepped back from the hug and touched her cheeks, hoping to calm her.

"They shot at me. There were two of them, Kenyon. What is going on here?"

Unless it was connected to what had happened to Beacon, the attack on her didn't make sense to him either. They knew that the woman who had taken Beacon had an accomplice because someone had picked her up when they were chasing her outside the campground. But why come after Raina, and how had they even found her? Or was the violence connected to the trafficking case with the brothers deciding to target people the task force cared about?

"Come on, I'll take you back home. We'll make arrangements for your car to be pulled out and towed."

Clearly still in shock, she gazed at her wrecked car for a long moment. "My deliveries."

"Raina, I'm not sure that has to be a priority right now. Maybe you can call your customers and let them know you'll bring them some other time."

"At least let me drop off the goodies at the B and B." Her voice still had that faraway quality. "It's just up the road."

"Okay, I'll help you with those. We can load all the orders into the patrol car."

"Aren't you on duty?"

"Daniel has given me a lot of leeway to adjust to my personal life."

The drive would give them a chance to talk more about what had happened once the shock wore off for Raina. He needed to go back to the house anyway to show Beacon the driver's license photo of Tanya. They walked to his vehicle together, and then he drove across the grass to her car.

By the time they loaded up the treats that were in containers with lids, the tow truck had shown up. Kenyon drove to the B and B, where Raina dropped off the goods. He walked to the door holding one of the containers for her. Her conversation with the owner was brief. It was clear that she was distracted.

The rain had turned to a drizzle when they got back in the car. She pressed her head against the seat and petted Peanut who sat between them. "Normally I would have stayed and visited, but needless to say, I don't feel like it."

"When you're ready, we can talk about what happened, but please don't feel any pressure."

Raina nodded but didn't say anything. He drove up the winding country road back toward the city.

"I do want to talk about it because I want you to catch the people who came after me." She'd regained her composure. He was glad that the spine of steel Raina had returned.

"Is that an order?" He spoke in a mock serious voice.

"Yes, Detective."

They both let out a small laugh.

"I haven't heard back from the patrol officer. He might still be in pursuit. Even if he doesn't catch them, we have a make and model for the car that ran you off the road. Can you tell me anything about the two people who came after you?"

"They both wore rain ponchos that covered most of them. The one that shot at me..." She closed her eyes for a moment.

He reached over and patted her leg. "Raina, if it's too soon, don't push yourself."

Peanut leaned close to her and licked her hand.

"No, I want to do this." She closed her eyes and drew a breath through her teeth. "I couldn't see their faces. They were far away, and the hoods covered them. I would say the one who came after me was a woman. And the other carried himself like a guy."

It had taken some effort for her to give him that information. As determined as she was, he wanted to give her time to recover. Silence seemed like the best option.

Raina spoke up after about ten minutes. "I wish I could tell you more about the two people who came after me so we would know if it had anything to do with what happened to Beacon."

Only Beacon had seen the woman for a sustained amount of time.

His radio crackled and the patrol officer came on the line.

"I've lost them."

His spirits sank. "Okay. At least we know the make and model of the car. Did you get a read on the license plate?"

"No. Never got close enough."

"I'm taking Raina back home." Kenyon signed off.

He came to the edge of town.

"Can we drop off another order? It's on the way at Cool Coffee."

"Sure, if you feel up to it."

She nodded. "I need to get as much work done as possible."

Raina had taken time away from work to help him with his memory recovery. When he'd disappeared, she'd moved out of the kitchen she'd customized to do her baking and worked out of his home. She'd made a lot of sacrifices. "I don't want you to worry about money. I have savings."

"We're not married, Kenyon. I think we should keep the finances separate. I'll take care of my own expenses."

He picked up on the hurt in her voice. "I know this situation is less than ideal. But if you move out, that might traumatize the boys."

"I'm with you on this, Kenyon. I want to do everything to protect Beacon and Austin."

He could feel the tension in the air as she spoke more intensely. Raina was entitled to a life and to be able to run her business like she needed to. They always seemed to come to an impasse with this conversation. "All I'm saying is that, as your friend, I don't want you to worry about money while you're helping care for the boys."

She stared out her window and spoke in a low voice. "Thank you."

He drove through town, finding a parking space a block from the coffee shop. As they pulled the containers out, he found himself looking around at the other cars.

They stepped into the coffee shop. Country music played at a low volume. Paintings of horses and wilderness landscapes hung on the walls. The scent of sugar and coffee hung in the air as people worked on computers or visited. A blonde woman who looked to be barely out of her teens ran the espresso machines. The older woman behind the counter waved at Raina and Kenyon. Raina walked confidently toward the counter but stopped, placing her container on a nearby table and clutching her stomach.

He rushed over to her. "Raina, what is it?"

She straightened up and stared toward the display counter. "I know how she figured out who I am."

SIX

With her stomach doing somersaults, Raina left her container on the table and hurried over to the display that was the same one she'd placed in the teahouse. A picture of her holding a tray of goodies, her face and name clearly visible. She slapped the back of the photo, so it was lying face down. Her picture was all over town in every place she supplied with baked goods. If the kidnapper had been in the same tour group as they were, she would have observed Raina interacting with Beacon.

The older woman, Mrs. Oberlain, came out from behind the counter at the same time that Kenyon reached Raina and placed a supportive hand on her back.

"Everything okay, Raina dear?" Mrs. Oberlain leaned toward her.

"We'll be all right," said Kenyon. "She's had a...hard day."

"Katie and I can go ahead and take the goods behind the counter." Mrs. Oberlain signaled to the blonde barista who had just set a coffee on the counter.

Kenyon leaned close to Raina, wrapping his hand around her arm above the elbow. "Let's go back to the car."

Raina flipped over the picture. "I think she saw my picture when she was at the teahouse right before I came with the delivery." Raina shook her head in disbelief. "She could have been waiting in the parking lot. Clive knew I was on my way to make a delivery. He might have told her that."

"I'm not sure what you're saying. Let's get back to the car, so we can talk in private."

When both of them were settled in the patrol car, Raina explained what the owner of the tea shop had said about a woman from out of town commenting on Raina's ad.

Kenyon thought for a moment. "That sounds plausible. She came to Plains City trying to figure out where Beacon lived, stopped at the teahouse and saw your picture."

Raina rested her head against the back of the seat. "That still doesn't explain why she and her accomplice came after me apparently with the intent to kill me." That reality chilled her to the bone. "Why not follow me until I led them home to where Beacon was?"

"We don't have a clear link between the people who came after you and the woman who took Beacon. Good police work requires we make that connection. The man we've not got any ID on could be Devin Lane. The woman Beacon saw could be helping him."

"Kenyon, I bake cakes for a living and teach Sunday school to six-year-olds. Who in my life would want me dead?"

A momentary smile spread across his face. "True, you don't lead a life that would attract criminals. First we need to confirm that the woman who took Beacon either is or isn't Tanya Starling." He turned the key in the ignition and pulled out onto the street.

Kenyon drove across town and pulled up in front of his home. As they headed up the walkway with Peanut, Raina could hear the sound of children running and laughing.

Kenyon pushed open the door. Trisha sat on the living room floor helping Beacon put together a project with interlocking blocks while Austin chased a giggling one-year-old Gabriel through the house. Chewy followed the running boys.

Something about the scene before her helped Raina take in a deep breath. Everyone here was safe…for now.

Trish rose to her feet. "Rain was coming down pretty hard. You both look a little rough around the edges. There's leftover mac and cheese with polish sausage if you want some."

Beacon stared down at his project, holding a block in each hand. "Trish makes good mac and cheese."

It warmed her heart that the boys had grown closer to Trish lately too. Her sister's ex, Gabriel's father, had abandoned Trish when he found out she was pregnant. It'd been heartbreaking to watch her sister go through that. After Raina and Trish had lost their parents in a car accident when they were nineteen and seventeen, they'd become even closer than they'd been as kids. Raina had been thrilled when Trish got engaged to West Cole in April.

A month ago, Trish and West had had a small wedding with Kenyon, Raina and some of the other officers and task force members they worked with present, along with a few friends. The day had been beautiful… And the whole time her eyes had been drawn to her gorgeous friend in his suit. She'd suppressed her feelings for Kenyon a long time ago. But losing him and then getting him back again had brought them back full force. She couldn't let herself fall for him like she had when they were young. There was too much at stake—they had the boys to think of now.

"The rain isn't the reason why we look so out of sorts," said Raina. She looked at Beacon, who was still focused on his project. "I'll explain later."

"I have to get back to work, but I would like to talk to Beacon for a minute," said Kenyon.

Trish looked concerned but seemed to take the hint that they couldn't talk in front of the boys. "Sounds good. I'll go deal with those other rapscallions."

While she and Kenyon sat down beside Beacon, she could hear the screams of delight coming from the next room as Trish wrestled with the boys and Chewy barked.

Beacon clicked a block into place, biting his lower lip in concentration. Peanut laid down close to the boy.

Kenyon glanced in Raina's direction. She could read the message in his expression. The slight raising of the eyebrow was his request for her help.

She scooted closer to the Beacon stroking Peanut's velvety ears. "What are you building here, Beacon?"

"It's going to be a restaurant where you can bring your dog and they can eat with you."

"That sounds like a great idea," said Kenyon.

They talked some more as Beacon explained what each lump of blocks was in his project until Kenyon let out a breath and scooted a little closer to his son. "Beacon, we have a picture to show you." He pulled his phone from a pocket in his uniform.

Raina rested her hand on Beacon's back. "Do you remember when that lady took you to the cabin?"

Beacon nodded. "She gave me a coloring book."

Nothing in Beacon's demeanor suggested talking about the kidnapping was upsetting him. "Yes," said Raina. "Daddy's going to show you a picture."

"We need for you to tell us if this is the woman who took you to that cabin." Kenyon moved the phone so Beacon could see it.

Placing his hand on his father's, Beacon stared for a long

moment while a crevice formed between his eyebrows. "Yes," he said. "That was the lady." He drew his attention back to his project. "I want to have a place where the dogs can get milkshakes."

"I bet that would be fun for them, Beacon," said Raina.

Kenyon and Raina exchanged a look. They had their answer. The kidnapper was Tanya Starling.

Feeling fired up and hopeful about the newly obtained evidence, Kenyon rested his back against the couch and watched his son carefully snap one plastic block into another. Almost from birth, Beacon was the quiet twin. Measured in his responses and seeming to think deeply about most things. Austin, on the other hand, was the loquacious one, always asking what-if questions and unafraid to talk to strangers or engage in social situations.

Now that they had a solid link to Tanya, it should be that much easier to track her down. The ID by Beacon would give law enforcement probable cause to take her in for questioning and to search her residence. Though he suspected that she might be hard to locate now that she knew law enforcement was on to her. They didn't know yet if the two people who had come after Raina were Tanya and her accomplice, but there was a high probability.

If so, that meant that Tanya was here in town. Having Trish stay at the house was good, but they would need to beef up protection even more.

His phone rang. Cheyenne. "I got to take this."

Raina gave him a pat on the arm. He loved the way they'd worked together, seeking to protect Beacon while still letting him do his job.

He rose to his feet and wandered out to the back porch for some privacy. "Yes."

"We got a possible ID on the man who attacked you at the amusement park. Pulled up driver's license photos based on the partial you got of the license plate. I can send the two possibilities to you."

"No need. I'll be back over to headquarters in fifteen minutes."

"Sounds good. I heard Raina ran into a little excitement."

"I'm just glad we got there on time. Did Zack and Jenna come up with any lead at the locations they searched?"

"No, yours was the strongest lead. We need to link this guy to the gun trafficking though. Once you give us a positive ID, Daniel is thinking the driver who got taken into custody with that sting last month and agreed to cooperate might be able to tell us if this guy has anything to do with the gun trafficking."

"Sounds good. Alan Tate might know something. There was no indication of guns present at Wild West Land. Makes me wonder if the guy was scouting possible locations. They could be moving the guns around the city to avoid detection."

"Could be. For sure, they're not going to stash the guns there now," said Cheyenne.

"See you in a few," he said.

He said goodbye and disconnected. When he turned around, Raina was standing in the doorway.

"You have to get back to work?" She rubbed her arm. The look in her eyes was not one he'd seen before. Even fearless Raina had a breaking point.

He stepped toward her, reaching out to touch her arm. "You'll be okay here?"

"Trish will stay with me."

Three children and two women, one an armed and

trained officer. "I'm going to request some more protection for you. I can stay if you want me to."

"Go to work. We'll be all right."

"All the same, I'll arrange for a patrol car to go by while I finish my shift, and Peanut can stay here with you. I'll just be at headquarters for the rest of the day."

She nodded. "I appreciate that."

He drew her into an embrace. "This has been a lot for you to endure."

She looked up at him. "It's the thought of anything bad happening to the boys that is the hardest to take."

His throat went tight. "I get that. They are my world now." His eyes warmed with tears.

"Go do your job. Catch that woman so she can't hurt us anymore." She reached up, touching his face and letting her finger trail from his temple to his cheek, something she had never done before. Then again, he'd never been moved to tears in front of her.

"We're in this together, Raina."

She nodded but took a step back, breaking the connection between them. "You go. Trish and I can handle things here. Peanut is always hyper-vigilant."

His head was still buzzing from the memory of her touch as he walked out to his vehicle. He got in and reached to turn the key in the ignition but then sat back.

Yes, there had been a spark of attraction between them just now, but they had been friends forever. What if they tried dating and it didn't work out? The friendship could be destroyed by it. That would blow the twins' world to pieces. He shook his head and stared at the ceiling.

God, why does everything have to be so hard?

He drove across town, stopping at the teahouse where

Raina delivered baked goods. Clive was wiping a table down when Kenyon entered.

"Detective Graves. Good to see you. Raina was by here earlier."

"I know. She mentioned that you had a customer from out of town who bought the last lemon bar."

With a confused look on his face, Clive straightened up and ran his hands through his thinning hair. "Yeah, sure."

"Do you think you might remember her if I showed you a picture?"

Clive shrugged.

Kenyon clicked through his phone, bringing up the driver's license photo of Tanya. He stepped closer so Clive could see it.

The older man stared at the photograph and then nodded. "Not the best picture. I think that could have been her." He looked closer and nodded. "Yeah, I think that was her."

Kenyon patted him on the back. "Thanks, Clive." He hurried out to his car. The woman who had come after Raina was most likely Tanya, along with her accomplice. The question was why. He'd have to answer that later. Right now, Raina could be in danger.

SEVEN

Raina pulled the cake out of the oven and set it on the counter. Peanut barked. It sounded like the dog was outside. Trying not to panic, she hurried to the kitchen window, she caught a glimpse of Austin running by with Peanut not far behind him. Sneaky little guy. How had he gotten outside without Trish noticing?

She ran to the kitchen door and flung it open. Austin was smacking a tree trunk with a stick. He'd tied a hoodie around his neck like it was a cape. He was playing superhero again.

"You need to get inside." She ran toward him trying to hide the fear from her voice.

Peanut let out a single bark as if to say she was doing her best to keep track of the children.

Austin scowled and crossed his arms. "But it stopped raining."

She held out her hand to him. They couldn't continue to do this much longer. Little boys needed to run and play and feel the sun on their skin.

"I know, honey."

"Why do I have to stay inside? That lady wants Beacon."

His statement stabbed through her. The boy understood more than she realized. But he hadn't made the connection that he looked exactly like his brother. It wasn't clear if Tanya realized Beacon was a twin. Austin had stayed with Kenyon and Beacon with her during the tour, so Tanya might not have seen them together. "Let's just go in. You can help me frost the cake."

Austin's face brightened. "Do I get to lick the paddle when we're done?"

"Of course."

The bribe worked. Austin took her hand with Peanut trailing behind him. Raina led him toward the kitchen door. Just before they entered, she gazed above the four-foot fence that enclosed the backyard, where she saw a Plains City patrol car go by.

She was grateful that Kenyon had arranged for an extra degree of protection. When he'd called to tell her that the woman at the teahouse matched Tanya's description, it sent chills down her spine.

After she finished her baking with Austin's help, she straightened up the kitchen and set the table for dinner. The sky had already begun to turn gray. It got dark early this time of year.

Once dinner was over and the three boys were settled in the living room watching a movie with the dogs, Trish and Raina sat in the kitchen sipping decaffeinated coffee. Raina glanced at the clock. "Kenyon should be off shift by now." She checked her phone. "Looks like he sent me a text."

Delayed. Got to question that guy the team took into custody last month. Everything okay there?

"He's going to be late getting home," she said to Trisha, then texted back.

Everything is fine and dandy here. Patrol car has gone by several times. Peanut is on duty. See you soon.

She looked up from her phone. Trisha stared at her. "What?"

Trisha took a sip of her coffee. "You always smile any time you text him."

"So?" Trisha was the only one who knew about Raina's feelings for Kenyon.

"Have you had a chance to talk about what the future looks like for the two of you?"

"Not really. We both want to do what is best for the boys. That's about as far as we seem to get before things get tense." Raina tried to keep her voice steady, but she knew she couldn't hide the heartbreak and anxiety Kenyon's indecisiveness was causing from her sister.

Trish leaned in and covered her sister's hand. "You can't keep living like this forever in this state of limbo."

"I know that. But Kenyon has been through a lot. Losing his wife and then not knowing who he was for all those months... I just don't think it's fair to put pressure on him."

"I understand. I know West's stress level is up because of the task force. I'm sure it affects Kenyon too in addition to everything else he's dealing with." Trisha stared out the window where the sky had grown dark. "Do you think he loves you...as more than a friend?"

Raina let out a heavy breath, remembering that spark of energy she'd felt between them when she'd touched his face. She had been the one to step away from the magnetic pull of his gaze. "I think that both of us are a little afraid of destroying what we have together."

Their conversation was interrupted by the sound of Peanut barking at the front door.

"Something's up. That's a warning bark." Trish rose from her chair. "I'll go check it out."

Raina's heart beat a little faster. "I'll go be with the kids." She glanced over her shoulder as Trish stepped outside gun in her hand and Peanut by her side.

Peanut's frantic barking came through the closed door. Raina rushed over to the children.

"Go to your room and lock the door. Take Gabriel."

Austin opened his mouth to protest.

"I said go."

All three boys scrambled toward their bedroom with Chewy following. Once the kids were safe in their room, Raina ran to the kitchen window. She couldn't see Peanut, but she was barking more intensely than ever. A shadow rushed by the window. Not her sister, someone dressed in black. Someone was in the yard. Raina grabbed her phone from where she'd set it on the table.

She rushed toward the front door with her phone in front of her face so she could dial 911. Had something happened to Trish?

The operator's crisp voice came across the line. "911. What is your emergency?"

She reached for the doorknob. "Someone's in my yard. My sister, a Plains City officer, may be hurt—"

A tremendous force hit the side of her head and then whirled her around. Her body collided with a piece of furniture, and she heard a crashing sound as she crumpled to the floor. As she lay on her stomach, out of breath, the figure dressed in dark clothes towered over her. She closed her eyes and dropped her head, faking unconsciousness. Her hope was that if the attacker thought she was incapacitated she'd be left alone.

"I'll get you later," a female voice said in a raspy whisper.

A second later, she heard retreating footsteps.

Dizzy from the blows she'd sustained, Raina lifted her head. Feeling disoriented, she pushed herself to her feet. She didn't see where her phone had fallen. Had she been on the phone long enough for law enforcement to pinpoint the address she'd called from?

A noise down the dark hallway attracted her attention. She stepped softly, trying not to make any sound. The dark figure was rattling the doorknob. She knocked and whispered, "Joey, it's me. Open the door."

"No," Raina yelled as maternal instinct kicked in, and she dove for the woman who was trying to take Beacon again.

The woman turned, pulling a small pistol from her pocket. "Get back. He's mine. Not yours."

Raina dove for the open door of her bedroom as the shot was fired. She could hear Tanya knocking on the door. At first her voice was soft, almost a whisper. "Joey, please let me in. It's going to be okay." Her voice became louder and more insistent as she rattled the doorknob. "I said open this door."

Raina heard a window breaking and the boys screaming. The sounds of the boys experiencing such terror made her whole body shake. Tanya's accomplice must be trying to get to the boys via their bedroom window. Raina gritted her teeth. Gun or no gun, she needed to save those boys. She angled her head so she could see up the hallway. Tanya's attention was focused on the door. She eased out into the hallway and rushed toward the other woman.

Tanya raised her gun again but was not able to fire a shot before Raina rammed into her chest and then headbutted her. While Tanya was stunned from the attack, Raina reached for the wrist that held the gun and slammed it against the wall. The gun fell on the floor and slid a few feet from the force of impact.

Tanya grabbed Raina's hair at the same time that she kicked the back of her knees. Raina went down, but she pulled Tanya with her. Tanya slammed Raina's head against the floor.

For a brief moment, she stared at Raina. Teeth gritted, face tight. The look of wildness in her eyes was of a woman who was clearly unhinged.

"Should have taken care of you first." Tanya all but spat out her words.

Sirens sounded in the distance. Tanya lifted her head. Raina breathed a sigh of relief. The house had been located through the emergency call she'd made.

Faced with the arrival of the police, Tanya pushed herself to her feet, turned and ran out the back door.

Out of breath and feeling dizzy, Raina pulled herself together and crawled the short distance to the locked door.

Please let them be safe.

"It's Raina. It's okay now. You can open the door."

She heard the padding of little feet and the twisting of the knob. The door opened. She fell to her knees and gathered Austin into her arms. Beacon and Gabriel ran toward her as well. "It's okay now. You're safe."

"There was a man at the window," said Beacon.

"He was trying to get in," said Austin. "We threw things at him."

She lifted her head to the window where the glass was broken. A large piece and several shards were scattered across the floor. She hugged them all tighter. "You were so brave and smart."

"I was scared," said Austin.

"I know, honey."

She heard her sister's voice behind her. Peanut was with her. "I'm tried to fight them off. Is everyone okay here?" Gabriel held his hands up, and Trish picked up her son. "I saw someone moving around the yard. I didn't realize there were two of them. One of them came up behind me and beaned me on the head while I was trying to stop the other one. I lost consciousness. Peanut stayed with me the whole time."

Down the hallway, she could see sirens flashing in the living room window. Kenyon entered the house and rushed toward them. The tension eased out of her body when she saw him. His expression relaxed when he saw that they were safe.

He fell to his knees and gathered all three of them into a hug.

Raina relished the moment of closeness and connection, knowing that it wouldn't last. It was clear that it wasn't safe for them to stay in the only home the boys had ever known. They'd lost their mother and for a while their father, and now they would be torn out of the house that was no longer a place of safety.

Seeing that his sons and Raina were unharmed had almost made his knees buckle. When the 911 call came in and the dispatcher had honed in on the fact that a police officer was down and recognized the address, she'd called Kenyon. He'd jumped in his vehicle and drove across town with a sick feeling in his stomach.

His had been the second car to arrive on the scene. The other had given chase to a car zooming up the street several blocks away.

When he peered in their room, he saw that the boys' backpacks were still packed from the aborted weekend at Wind Cave. His gaze landed on the broken window and the pieces of glass on the floor. Rage coursed through him at the thought of anyone trying to harm his sons.

Raina gave Trish a look, some sort of secret signal between sisters.

Trish shifted Gabriel in her arms. "Come on, guys. Let's go in the kitchen."

Austin glanced at Kenyon and Raina. "What for?"

"Raina and your daddy need to talk, and we're going to have ice cream." Austin nodded. Beacon followed them toward the kitchen with a backward glance toward Raina and Kenyon.

Kenyon lifted his chin. The stricken expression on Beacon's face made Kenyon's chest tight. It was clear the events of the evening had shaken the boy. "I'll come hang out with you guys in just a minute."

Beacon nodded and followed the others down the hallway.

Once he heard Trisha's attempt at positive chatter coming from the kitchen, he stepped closer to Raina.

To his surprise, she fell into his arms. He wrapped his arms around her. She seemed to melt against him.

"Oh, Kenyon, I'm so afraid for Beacon. And Austin too. We don't know if Tanya realizes Beacon has a twin."

He relished the hug for a moment longer before stepping away. "Unless they catch those two tonight, we need to leave here."

"I agree, but where will we go?"

"It'll take at least a day to set up a safe house that's close. I know you want to do your work, but you're a target too for whatever reason. I don't think you should be out in the open."

"I think I know why I'm a target. The way Tanya talked tonight. I think I'm a threat to her messed up reality. She probably thinks I'm Beacon's mom."

Kenyon nodded. "That might be."

Raina shuddered and crossed her arms over her body.

"What she said tonight implied that she intended to kill me. I guess I don't have a lot of options."

"Like I said before, I'll help you out financially."

"Everything is getting so messy. I don't want to have to rely on you financially. I can't let my business go under."

Kenyon nodded. She had spoken more clearly and directly than ever before. There was just so much potential harm to the boys with any choice they made, but a great deal was at stake for Raina as well.

"I appreciate all the sacrifices you're making, Raina."

"I never thought of it that way, that it was a sacrifice. I love those boys. I want the best for them."

Her words warmed his heart. Up until he showed back up in their lives, she had thought she would be raising them alone. His return had to have been jarring, upsetting the life she thought she was going to have after having mourned his loss. "I know we have to figure something out. Right now though, both the boys and you need more protection."

She nodded. "That's the most pressing issue. What do you suggest we do? Where can we go?"

"Maybe we can stay at a hotel tonight and get an officer to watch the door while I stay inside with you guys."

Raina nodded. "I'll throw some of my things together."

"It looks like the boys are still packed from the weekend. I didn't unpack my duffel yet either."

"I'll grab it for you." She turned to go but then looked back at him. "How much do we tell them?"

"I know they're only three, but I'm sure they understand the threat after tonight. Let's be honest but careful in our word choice."

She squeezed his upper arm. "Go hang out with your son. He needs you."

Raina had seen that earlier look on Beacon's face as

well. He appreciated her strength and her deep conviction to protect the boys—mind, body and soul.

She hurried up the hallway to her room.

Kenyon was headed toward the kitchen when there was a knock on the door. He could see through the window by the door that it was a patrol officer. He rushed to open it.

"Did they catch them?"

"No word yet." He turned slightly toward the street. "I think I know how she found you. Right before we got this call, there were two different reports of people describing creepy behavior from a woman matching Tanya's description or a car parked by their house for a long time."

"Why is that important?"

"Both people filing the complaints had the last name of Graves."

There were a lot of Graves in this town, some of whom he was only distantly related to. She'd clearly looked up addresses of anyone with that name and was waiting to spot Beacon or Raina. Which meant Tanya knew Beacon's full name. "She must have gotten Beacon's last name from the Amber Alert."

"If that's the case, she's very methodical and driven," said the officer.

"It's clear she's unstable and delusional," said Kenyon. "I need to go hang out with my kids. We're going to a hotel for the night. Do you mind following us in your patrol car?"

"Let me get permission from Captain Ross."

"And then I need an officer outside the room for the night," said Kenyon. "I'd ask Trisha or West, but she got conked on the head earlier and I know West will want to be home with her and Gabriel tonight." And his colleagues at the task force were all chasing down leads on the gun smugglers.

The officer nodded. "I might be able to do that until the end of my shift. I'll see what the department can set up for you."

Kenyon turned and entered the warm glow of the kitchen, where the boys sat around the table eating ice cream.

Trish gathered Gabriel into her arms. "I need to be heading home."

"There's an ambulance outside, Trish," he said. "You might want to get checked out."

"I will," said Trish.

Raina entered the kitchen holding the backpacks, the duffel and her overnight bag. She gave her sister a sideways hug. "I'm glad you were here tonight."

"I just wish I hadn't let those guys get a jump on me."

Raina squeezed her sister's hand. "If you hadn't been here, it could have been so much worse."

After Trish left, Beacon pushed his empty ice cream bowl away from him. He pointed to the backpacks. "Are we leaving because of the bad lady?"

"Yes, we need to go someplace she can't find us."

Beacon became visibly upset, biting his lower lip while tears formed in his eyes. "I told her my name is not Joey."

Kenyon picked up Beacon and let the boy cry against his chest while he made soothing sounds and stroked his hair.

Raina sat down beside Austin, who crawled into her lap. "I know this is scary."

As he watched her hold Austin, he realized there was no way he could get through this without her.

Once the boys calmed down, he taped up the broken window being careful not to touch where the intruder could have left prints knowing that the forensics team would come and dust for them later. Raina helped him load the boys along with Peanut and Chewy into his car. The officer followed them in his patrol car to a hotel across town that he knew allowed pets.

They got to the first-floor room and settled in. The patrol officer sat in the hallway outside their door. The hotel room was a suite with a bedroom with two beds and a sitting room with a pull-out sofa. He and Raina worked to get the boys settled down. After Kenyon read them a story, Raina tucked them into the queen-size bed, kissing each one of them on the forehead. Chewy had already jumped up onto the bed to sleep close to the twins.

"I'm going to try to get some sleep too," she whispered.

"You can have the other bed in the room with the boys. I'll take the fold-out couch." He wandered into the sitting room with Peanut following him.

Despite being exhausted, Kenyon knew he wouldn't sleep much. He took off his gun belt and unbuttoned his shirt. He stared out the window, watching the city below and the lights of the cars on the road. This room provided a view of the parking lot, so he could see people coming and going. Peanut stood beside him, propping her front legs on the window so she could look out. Kenyon stroked the dog's head. "We're on guard duty together, aren't we?"

The dog wagged her tail.

He pulled his gun from the holster so it would be within easy reach. When he sat down on the couch, Peanut took up a position at his feet. Though she lay in a resting position, her head was up and alert to her surroundings. The thing about K-9s is they never really let themselves go off duty. He still had a view of the window from where he sat. Kenyon took in a breath and settled in for what he assumed would be a long night.

EIGHT

Raina awoke to the sound of Kenyon talking on the phone in the next room. The boys were still asleep. She rose and wrapped her robe around her.

Kenyon sat in the chair. His hair was still wet from a shower, and he was dressed in a button-down shirt and jeans. Peanut sat at his feet.

He smiled when he saw Raina, but the shadows under his eyes indicated he hadn't slept much.

"Thanks for the info, Cheyenne," he said into the phone. "Glad we were able to make a connection to the gun trafficking with that guy." He pushed the disconnect button and looked at Raina. "I just made some coffee. Want some?"

"Sure."

"There's a continental breakfast buffet in the lobby. I grabbed a few things for you and the boys. I don't think it would be good to have them out in public to eat."

She focused her attention on several breakfast bars and muffins on the table and grabbed a blueberry muffin and a napkin.

He set a cup of coffee down in front of her along with two sugar packets.

"That was Cheyenne on the phone?"

"Yes, she found out a little more about Tanya." The tone of his voice grew dark as he sat down. "Some uniformed officers went to her last known residence, which was the Starling family home. She must have inherited it when her parents died. No sign that she'd been there in the last few days, but the officers tracked down neighbors who Cheyenne talked to over the phone."

She shook the sugar packets and then ripped them open. "So what did Cheyenne find out about her? Not good, I take it."

"She's been a troubled person since her brother's death. She may have been unstable before that and the accident pushed her over the edge. It seems she liked to set fire to things but nothing reaching the level of a felony. Those juvenile records were sealed, so she was still able to get into the army."

Raina drew her breath through her teeth. "Did she have anything to do with her brother's death?"

"No, that was clearly an accident. The kid got away from the tour group and wandered through a roped-off area. The report said Tanya was with her parents when Joey went missing. All the members of the family were looking for him at the time he was found."

"Why now after all these years is she trying to bring back her dead brother?"

Kenyon shrugged. "The parents died less than a year ago. According to the neighbors the officers spoke to, the mom and dad were the ones that kind of kept Tanya in check. Their deaths might have made her want to try to get her family back in some twisted way."

"What about her accomplice? The guy that broke the window last night."

"Still trying to get an ID on him. Forensics didn't find and usable prints around the window at my house. Neighbors didn't notice any man hanging around Tanya's house."

"I wonder if the boys saw him clearly last night," said Raina.

"I'd rather not bring it up with them unless there's no other option. Maybe there is some other way we can figure out who he is."

"That would be best." Raina took a sip of her coffee. "You're making progress with the gun trafficking thing too?"

"Yes." Kenyon grabbed one of the granola bars and ripped it open. "Last month in a sting, the team caught a low-level driver who agreed to cooperate. He identified the big man I chased in Wild West Land as someone he'd worked with before. We think the big guy might have been scouting locations to stash some guns."

"That does sound like good news." The scene between her and Kenyon felt very domestic, as if they were a married couple, and she was trying to be encouraging and supportive about his work like a wife would do. She could almost fool herself into believing that it was so.

"Hopefully, we'll get a break in the case today."

She shifted in her seat. "You're going back to work? I thought maybe you had the day off."

"Jenna is going to swing by and give me a ride to the to get my police vehicle and I need to grab some files I left there. I'll leave the car here for you in case you need it for whatever reason."

Something about him being gone made her anxious in a way she had never felt before. Hadn't their friendship worked because of her independent spirit? "When are they moving us to the safe house?"

Her need to have him around had shifted since his return in a way she didn't fully understand. Certainly, it was connected to both of them taking care of the twins, but there was something deeper going on. She was becoming dependent on him, and she wasn't sure if she liked that. In the few romantic relationships she'd had, the men had always cited her fierce independence as the reason they broke up with her. They used other words, like cold and standoffish. In a way, she'd been forced to not depend on others. After her parents died, she'd taken care of both herself and Trish when she was barely nineteen.

He rested his hand on top of hers. "Hopefully that will happen before the day is over. A police officer is going to continue to stay outside your door. Trish is going to help with the transfer to a safe house if we can make it happen today."

She stared down at his hand that covered hers. "And what about you, Kenyon? What will your role be in getting us to the safe house?"

Her voice sounded a little too needy or accusatory.

She detected a change in his demeanor—a slight flicker in his eyes and expression like sunlight suddenly covered by clouds. "I intend to get back here as quickly as I can." He leaned toward her. "We're in this together, Raina."

His words quelled all her fears. She leaned closer to him. She could get lost in the blue of his eyes and stay suspended in this moment forever.

Chewy barked in the next room. The chatter of little boys waking up filled the air. They both pulled away at the same time as Austin burst into the room with Chewy scrambling behind him. His dark hair was a wild mess, sticking out at all angles.

"You hungry?" Kenyon grabbed one of the granola bars and tossed it in Austin's direction.

Austin caught the package. He looked at it for a moment. "I don't like blueberry. What else you got?"

Raina pointed at the food on the table. "Looks like strawberry and apricot or you can have a muffin."

After moving toward the table, Austin wiggled his mouth while he considered his choices. "Strawberry, I guess."

Kenyon scooted the granola bar in his direction. Beacon emerged from the bedroom rubbing his eyes. While Austin tended to hit the ground running in the morning, Beacon needed to wake up slowly.

"Hey, buddy." Kenyon held his arms out toward Beacon, who wandered over and crawled into his lap.

"We got granola bars." Austin spoke as he shifted his weight back and forth. A granola morsel shot out of his mouth.

"Austin, don't talk with your mouth full." She couldn't hide her amusement at his antics.

"Sorry." He swung side to side and took another bite.

By the time Kenyon's DGTF colleague Jenna, with her K-9 partner, Augie, knocked on the door and told Kenyon she was ready to go, the boys were in the other room getting dressed.

"I'll just be a minute," said Kenyon. "Got to say good-bye to my boys."

"I'll wait outside." Jenna closed the door.

Raina listened to Kenyon wrestling with the twins in the next room, making them laugh before saying goodbye. "I gotta go to work, guys."

"Oh, Dad," Austin protested.

"Yes, that's how it has to be. Now come here and get a hug." A moment later, he was standing in the doorway. He turned back toward the bedroom. "Take care of each other and Raina."

"We will." The boys spoke in unison.

He walked across the floor and stood a few feet from her. "Like I said, I'll get back here as fast as I can."

She nodded, realizing the moment had become awkward. Should she hug him goodbye? "I hope work goes good for you." She reached over and bumped her fist on his shoulder. "Stay safe out there. Isn't that what cops say to each other?"

What was going on? They'd hugged each other in the past without it being anything more than a way to express their friendship.

"Sure." He grabbed his gun belt. "See ya." With Peanut heeling beside him. He headed for the door without making eye contact, but she noticed the blush in his cheeks.

Maybe Kenyon had started to see her in a more romantic way, the whole thing made him uncomfortable.

Raina stared at the closed door. She wondered if after all this was over and Tanya was in custody, if she should move out and try to be in the boys' lives as much as possible until Kenyon made up his mind.

For now, she needed to stay with the twins and under police protection. Her life and the safety of the boys depended on it.

As he rode in the car with Jenna, Kenyon felt as though his insides had been stirred with a stick. Peanut sat between them.

Jenna glanced his way. "Everything all right?"

"Yeah, sure. Why?"

"'Cause you look like you're about to come down with the flu or something."

He pressed his palms against his cheeks. Is that how he looked to the world? "No, I'm not getting sick…physically anyway."

"What do you mean?"

Maybe he did need to talk to someone about all of this. A female perspective might help him sort through his feelings. Normally, Raina played that role in his life. "Raina's been my friend forever, right? She helped me wrestle my 4-H pig out of the mud and get him cleaned up for the fair. I've never seen her back off or show fear on a mountain bike ride. She gave me advice when I dated before I got married. I've always just thought of her as my buddy."

"But something's different?"

"I feel like I'm seeing her in a whole new light since I

came back—" How had his feelings changed? He wasn't even sure.

"And you…care about her in a deeper way?"

"Something like that." The feelings of attraction were new. A hug was no longer just a hug. Being close to her made him feel lightheaded. Plus, she'd been great with his boys. "Seeing how she stepped up for the twins when I was gone and helped me with my memory recovery… She's a pretty incredible woman."

"One thing's for sure. You don't want to make any big changes until this Tanya person is caught," said Jenna.

"Why?"

"Maybe all these new feelings are just being fueled by the perilous circumstances you're under. I've seen it happen before." She clicked the signal and turned onto the street that led back to his house.

Kenyon hadn't thought of it that way, but maybe it was true. "So don't do anything big and bombastic until we're past this crisis?"

"That would be my advice." She slowed as she got closer to Kenyon's house. "It wouldn't hurt for you to tell her how you feel."

"First I have to figure that out." What he feared more than anything was losing Raina's friendship. He didn't think his heart could take one more loss.

Jenna pulled into the driveway by his police vehicle.

Kenyon pushed open the door. "Thanks for the ride."

"I'll be here for a hot minute. I've got some texts to answer."

He commanded Peanut to jump down.

Kenyon hurried inside after unlocking the front door. He rushed down the hallway and grabbed the files he needed. As he walked back, he glanced into the boys' room, gazing at the taped-up window—then at the other window.

His attention was drawn to the street beyond the fenced-in backyard. A man sitting in a car looked in the direction of the house.

It wasn't illegal to park on the street and look at houses.

Kenyon carefully sidled into the room and ducked down below the window out of view. Peanut pressed in close to him. He peered just above the windowsill. The car was parked at an angle where he couldn't see the license plate. The man never got out of the car even after a few minutes. Instead, he drew a pair of binoculars up to his eyes, watching Kenyon's house.

That had to be Tanya's accomplice. They couldn't arrest him, but they could take him in for questioning.

With Peanut by his side, he hurried out the front door as Jenna backed out of the driveway. She must have seen the panic in Kenyon's expression and rolled down the window as Kenyon ran toward her.

"Guy in a white sedan around the block with a view to the back of the house acting suspicious." Kenyon pointed up the street. "Go around behind him. I'll get in my car and head him off in the other direction in case he decides to take off."

After Peanut jumped up in the kennel, Kenyon got into his car and shifted into Reverse. Just as he was about to turn the corner on the street where the car was parked, Jenna's voice came through the radio. "Suspect pulled out when I turned up the street. Headed south on Lawson. Lost visual on him."

He was closer to that street than Jenna was. "Got it." Kenyon did a quick turn in. "I'm in pursuit."

"I think he freaked when he saw my patrol car. He took off just when I would have become visible in his side view mirror."

"Sounds like the action of someone who's up to something." Kenyon spoke into the radio.

Still searching, Kenyon rolled through the residential streets until it met up with a commercial part of town. He drove past a used car lot and a fast-food place, not seeing the car anywhere. He picked up his radio. "Anything?"

"No sign of him. I went up and down several streets, thinking he might have pulled over somewhere."

Kenyon's gaze moved up and down the street one more time before he responded. "Let's head back to the station." It looked as if Tanya and her accomplice still thought they were at the house. The accomplice may have been watching for signs of activity. It was just a matter of time before they figured out Raina and Beacon were no longer staying there. Maybe they could set a trap for Tanya before they figured that out. Make it look like they were still there and then wait with several other officers for her to break into the house again.

He'd have to run the idea by Captain Ross and maybe get some help from the task force.

Speaking of, Daniel's voice came through the radio. "How far out are you?"

For the moment, Kenyon would have to shift his focus to the DGTF case. "One minute away."

"I'm sitting in the station parking lot in an unmarked car. Brandon has been spotted entering and eating at an establishment known as the Silver Spur. Zach Kelcey and a Plains City officer are going to help me run a tail on him when he comes out. I could use an extra set of eyes in the car."

"Can do." A second later, he pulled into the station parking lot, spotting Daniel's car right away. He parked and got Peanut out of the kennel.

While an extra set of eyes is nice when running a tail, Daniel's invitation was probably more about getting Kenyon up to speed about how the task force worked as a team and giving him a soft break-in to being back at work after all that had gone on.

After walking the short distance to Daniel's car, Kenyon settled into the passenger seat of the unmarked vehicle. Dakota must've been at the kennel in back of the building. Peanut sat on Kenyon's lap.

Daniel pulled out of the lot. "We've already got one officer inside the restaurant who will let us know when Brandon is done eating so we can be ready for him. Hopefully, this time he'll lead us to where the guns are being stored."

"So for sure the guns have arrived in Plains City?"

"That's what Alan Tate was able to get out of his contact within the organization, but exact location is still a mystery," said Daniel. "Tate said they were in the habit of moving the guns around quite a bit to avoid detection."

While all the intel revealed that the brothers were the ring leaders for the gun trafficking, they had to catch them in the act in order to arrest them. They seemed to be more hands-on of late. Maybe they were losing henchmen or maybe they were worried the job wouldn't be done right since the task force had been able to confiscate so many guns.

Zach and another local officer radioed that they were in place just as the Silver Spur came into sight.

While they waited, Kenyon filled in Daniel about his very personal case and shared his idea of setting up Tanya Starling. "I'm pretty sure the guy watching the house was Tanya's accomplice. That means they are looking for another opportunity, and they think that we're still there."

"That sounds like a good idea," said Daniel. "I'd be glad to help you with that. I'll explain to your captain."

"Getting this wrapped up and knowing the boys and Raina are safe would help me to put more energy into the trafficking investigation."

After about twenty minutes, the officer in the restaurant spoke in a low voice through his wire. "He's at the register."

Daniel started his car up. A moment later, Brandon came out the front door. His body language indicated that he was in hypervigilant mode—stiff shoulders and glancing side to side. He was a hulk of a man, short but muscular. His head looked like it rested on his shoulders. The driver had indicated that Brandon was not the smart brother. Hal was the one who made decisions and Brandon functioned more as an enforcer. All the interviews the team had done with people who knew Brandon, from ex-girlfriends to accomplices, indicated that he was a hothead.

Brandon got into his car and shut the door.

Daniel spoke into the radio. "Our man is on the move. Headed toward Truman Street."

"Got him." Zach's voice came through the radio.

Daniel pulled out onto the street at least thirty seconds after Zach slipped in behind Brandon's car.

A few seconds later the other officer's generic car was behind them but with two cars between them. The key to running a good tail was to tag team with the vehicles and to hang back so the target never caught on that he was being followed.

Zach's car slowed then turned on a side street. "I'm moving up," said Daniel. They switched off tailing Brandon through town while he stopped at a convenience store and then a bowling alley. Though the bowling alley had a closed sign hanging in the window, Brandon stepped through an unlocked door and disappeared inside.

Daniel parked on a side street while they waited for Brandon to come out of the bowling alley. Once Brandon came outside, he drove to a more industrial part of town with a lot of warehouses and machine shops.

The turn signal on Brandon's car blinked. Daniel radioed the others his location and then drove in the direction that Brandon had gone. They came to a two-story warehouse that appeared unused. The structure was in a sort of horse-shoe shape, with the parking lot being inside the horseshoe.

There was no sign of Brandon's car.

One end of the building looked like it might have an opening large enough for a car to get through, probably some sort of loading dock. There were several garage-sized doors on the lower level. They had only been seconds behind Brandon. It didn't seem like he would have had time to hide the car. Kenyon looked through the rear window, wondering if Brandon might have turned off somewhere before arriving at the warehouse. "Where did he go?"

"I don't know, but this would be a really good place to hide some weapons." Daniel shifted the car out of Park. "I don't like how boxed in we are here. Let the others know we're moving out."

Kenyon reached for the radio just as a rifle shot zinged through the air and hit the hood of the car. Heart pounding, Kenyon caught a flash of movement on the roof.

Several more shots were fired at the car as Daniel backed up.

Peanut sat up lifted her head and let out a single sharp bark.

A flutter of movement in his peripheral vision caused Kenyon to jerk his head toward the balcony where Peanut had been looking on the other side of the warehouse. It took a moment for him to process what he was seeing—a man stepping out of the shadows with an RPG on his shoulder.

"Get out of the car!" Kenyon screamed as he pushed open the door and rolled with Peanut in his arms. The explosion came a second later. Fire and heat surrounded Kenyon as he scrambled to his feet and ran. He had no way of knowing if Daniel had made it out of the car alive.

NINE

Kenyon's throat felt like it had been scraped with a hot knife. The exposed skin on his face and arms burned. He wheezed in air running toward the cover of a pile of tangled metal. Another rifle shot was fired from the roof, coming close to hitting him. Peanut tucked in close to him.

Daniel's car was a giant fireball.

The sound of sirens seemed muffled and far away. The other two officers must have seen the blast that the RPG created, even if they were blocks away.

Smoke filled the air and caused his eyes to sting as he looked out from behind the pile of metal. He could no longer see the shooter on the roof, and the balcony on the other side of the building was empty as well.

Where was Daniel?

Oh, God, let him be okay.

He saw flashing lights, then hands lifted him up from the ground. Zach had his face close to Kenyon's, saying something to him. Either he was so in shock he couldn't decipher the words, or his hearing had been affected by the explosive power of the RPG.

Two ambulances and two fire trucks pulled into the warehouse parking lot.

Tightness threaded through his chest when he still could

not see Daniel. He grabbed Zach's arm and mouthed Daniel's name. Zach's face drained of color as he shook his head.

Kenyon was led to the ambulance and handed off to an EMT who helped him onto the gurney inside. Peanut sat at his feet and licked his hand. The EMT said something about needing to open up his shirt to check for burns. He saw then that the sleeves of his shirt had been singed. His escape had been narrow.

Kenyon sat up and pulled off the blood pressure band the EMT had secured on him. He had to find Daniel. He needed to know if his task force leader, the man he considered a friend, had made it.

Firefighters, several more police officers and even some onlookers occupied the area around the burning car.

Then he saw a man bent over with two other officers all but holding him up. Daniel. Kenyon took in a breath of smoke-filled air. Daniel's clothes looked as if they had almost been blown off of him. His shirt was in shreds and his face was blackened.

Kenyon ran toward him, took him in his arms and hugged him. "Man, am I glad to see you." His voice had come back.

"You have no idea." Daniel's response came out in a hoarse whisper.

The EMT who had been in the ambulance led Kenyon back to it and ushered him inside again. After about ten minutes, Kenyon was sitting up with a blanket around his shoulders. Peanut nuzzled close to him beneath the blanket. He watched the second ambulance drive away.

Zach stuck his head in. "They're taking Daniel to the ER. He's got some second-degree burns on his arms that need to be taken care of."

Kenyon's hearing seemed to have recovered. "Looks like our traffickers are now dealing in RPGs." A frightening escalation. "This might have been a setup, a show of force." The intent had clearly been that both he and Daniel die in the attack. If the brothers had succeeded, other responding task force members and officers could have been harmed as well.

"I think they were trying to send us a message to back off," said Zach. "They must not be happy with how close we're getting to them with the investigation."

"All the more reason to work that much harder at catching them." This fight had always been personal to Kenyon. Realizing both he and Daniel could have perished made him even more determined to see this thing to the end.

Kenyon was transported to the hospital to be checked out in the ER. He insisted that Peanut be examined as well. While he waited in one of the curtained rooms, his thoughts turned to Raina. He needed to hear her voice. He pressed in her number.

"Hey."

"Kenyon. Is everything all right?"

With one word she'd picked up on his distress.

"Long story. I'm okay. That's what matters." He didn't want to upset her with the details. Just talking to her gave him back his equilibrium. "How are you and the boys doing?"

"They are getting a little stir crazy, but we'll survive. Do you want me to put them on?"

"Sure."

He could hear Raina calling the twins' names and then saying something that he couldn't discern. She came back on the line. "Beacon's asleep, but Austin wants to talk to you."

"Hi, Daddy."

"Hey, buddy."

"I had chili mac for lunch."

"Did you? That sounds yummy." He spoke with his son for a few minutes more, talking about nothing important but relishing the sound of his sweet voice.

"Bye, Daddy." Austin abruptly ended the conversation, probably because something else caught his attention.

Raina came back on the phone. "Trisha called me about an hour ago. The safe house should be ready for us before the day is over."

"That's good news. I intend to be there to help with that. I'll get in touch with her."

"I'm glad you called. It's good to hear your voice."

"Same here." He disconnected and stared at the phone for a long moment. Despite the emotional turmoil the explosion had caused, the conversation had given him a sense of peace.

The doctor came in and examined him. He had some bruises and scrapes but otherwise was okay.

"You are free to go and your dog seems okay as well," said the doctor. "That was quite a traumatic experience. If at all possible, why don't you take the rest of the day off."

"I'll see what I can do about that," said Kenyon.

When he stepped into the waiting room, with Peanut trailing beside him, Zach was sitting in one of the chairs. "Thought you might need a ride back to headquarters."

"Yeah, my car is there." Kenyon followed Zach through the ER doors out into the sun. "Any word on Daniel?"

"He was released. He wanted to come back to work, but the doctors advised him to take the rest of the day off."

"Same here." Kenyon got into the passenger seat. As they drove back toward headquarters, he phoned Daniel.

"How ya doin', my friend?"

"None the worse for wear," Daniel responded. He could hear the sound of a little girl laughing and talking in the background. "I've been advised by the doctor to take the day off."

"Do that," said Kenyon. "Doctor told me the same thing. It will give me a chance to help with transporting Raina and the boys."

"That's not really taking the day off then, is it?"

"I don't know how it would be classified. I want to ensure their safety."

"Well, it's important to take care of your family."

"Yes," said Kenyon as the word *family* echoed through his head.

Silence fell between the two men. Perhaps Daniel was thinking about his own family. Joy's mother, Serena, was the product of his father having an affair and then choosing not to be a part of Serena's life. Though he came from wealth, Daniel had chosen a much more humble lifestyle and profession.

"I think I would like to go through with the sting to catch Tanya tonight if that's all right. You might not feel up to it. I'm sure I can recruit some colleagues from the PCPD or the task force."

"No, I'm all in on that," said Daniel.

"Looks like neither one of us is actually taking the day off."

Daniel laughed. "You got me. I'm home, but I'm sitting in front of my laptop rereading the reports on the trafficking case. We've been tailing Hal and Brandon for days. The guns have to be someplace they frequent. I've got a search warrant pending to look in the warehouse where we were ambushed. I have a feeling though that even if the guns were there at one time, they're gone by now."

"Yes, there is a good chance they're moving the shipment around until they can get it out of Plains City," Kenyon said. "Take care. I'll be in touch later in the day."

Zach dropped Kenyon off. He and Peanut jumped in his car and headed across town to be with Raina and the boys. Work was important, but right now he was grateful to be able to be with the people he cared about most.

He prayed that Tanya had not yet figured out that they had left the house.

Raina sat reading her Bible, grateful that the boys had finally gone down for a nap. Each of them had only had one toy and one small stuffed animal stashed in their backpacks. A truck for Austin and a drawing paper and crayons for Beacon. She didn't want to use her phone too much to entertain them, so she had had to be inventive about the games they played.

First, they pretended that the beds were boats surrounded by shark-infested waters and pirates. Then they built a tent out of blankets and went camping.

Though she was exhausted from the intensity of trying to entertain two three-year-old boys in a confined space, it was a good kind of tired.

A police officer had remained outside the door all day.

There was a soft knock on the door and then Kenyon stepped in. Seeing him lifted her spirits, though he looked really tired. She wondered what had happened today. She had heard longing in his voice when he'd called her earlier. She put her finger perpendicular to her mouth and then pointed to the bedroom.

"They're finally asleep," she whispered.

He nodded and sat down beside her, keeping his voice low as he spoke. "I just talked to Trisha on the phone. She's on her way over. The safe house is ready."

Raina nodded. They'd been safe here for the time being, but that probably couldn't last long-term. Tanya seemed pretty determined to take the child she viewed as her brother. "Please tell me the place has a backyard with a high fence. Those boys really need some outdoor activity."

"I have no idea what has been set up." His hand rested on hers. "This has been a lot to deal with alone. I'll help wear them out, so they are tired by bedtime."

"Thank you." She was grateful Kenyon had an understanding of what her day had been like.

"Raina, I do appreciate all that you've done. I… It's good to be here with you and the boys."

"I like being with them. I thought I was going to be their mom, remember." Without a body, it would have taken seven years for Kenyon to be declared legally dead, but she had already had the adoption papers drawn up. Her throat grew tight. "It's hard to give up that idea. Hard to stop being a mom. You don't just turn those feelings off, you know." She loved the twins with a mother's love. And if Kenyon could only get beyond his pain, she knew she could love him as his wife.

Kenyon's voice filled with compassion. "I never meant for life to unfold this way. For you to have to go through all this. I didn't think Monique would die or all this other stuff would happen."

She closed her Bible. They were both tied up in knots over this whole thing. "Well, you know what I always say. You make a plan, and God makes a plan. Guess who's the head of the planning committee."

He rose to his feet and ran his hands through his dark hair. "I do remember you saying that."

She stood up as well and stepped toward him. "This is happening for a reason."

"I know, but sometimes you only see the reason in retrospect." His voice filled with angst.

She stepped closer, patting the back of his shoulder. He turned to face her, looking at her with those blue eyes. Something about him seemed...different. Maybe something had happened at work that he wasn't willing to share.

Had the explosion that took his memory never happened, she wondered if somewhere down the line Kenyon could have seen her as romantic material. It had only been a little over two years since his wife's death. As it was, his losses were so numerous he probably couldn't even consider the possibility of dating and love.

Once again, she felt a check in her spirit not to put pressure on him. "I hope this transport goes okay today."

"Far as we know, Tanya still thinks we're at the house. There was a man watching it earlier who we think was her accomplice."

"But you don't know for sure?"

He shook his head. "Daniel and I are going to try to set up a sting to catch her tonight. I'm going to take my car back there and park it in the driveway, so it looks like we're home. Your car should have already been dropped off from the shop."

"I hope that works. This whole thing could be over by tomorrow."

There was another knock at the door and Trisha stepped inside. "Are you guys ready?"

"The boys are still asleep," said Raina.

As if on cue, she heard the sound of Austin stirring and

immediately launching into a story that he must be telling his sleeping brother. Beacon wouldn't be able to stay asleep for long.

Trisha smiled. "Sounds like you won't have to wake them."

"Trish and I worked this out earlier," said Kenyon. "You and the boys and the dogs will ride with me in the car."

Trish stepped toward her sister. "I came in my personal vehicle. We're not taking any patrol cars. That would call attention to us."

As she and Kenyon got the boys packed up and ready to go, tension threaded through Raina, making her stomach feel like it was tied up in knots. Kenyon didn't know for sure if Tanya still thought they were at the house. She might have been watching the PCPD building and followed him or one of the other officers here.

When they opened the hotel door, the police officer stood up from the chair he'd been sitting on. "I'll go out with you guys before I head back to the station."

Three police officers and a K-9 surrounded Raina and the boys as they walked down the hallway through a back door and out into the parking lot. The sky was already turning gray. It got dark around dinnertime in the fall.

Kenyon buckled Austin into his car seat while Raina helped Beacon.

"Are we going where the bad lady can't find me?"

She pressed her fingers against his cheek. "Yes." She ran her fingers through his dark hair. "We want you to be safe."

He hugged the stuffed buffalo he held closer to his chest. "I love you, Raina." When Kenyon had been presumed dead, she had toyed with the idea of telling the boys they could call her mom but thought it might be too soon after losing both their parents. Now she was glad for that decision. Hearing that sweet voice call her mom would have made everything harder.

"Love you too." She kissed him on the forehead. When she looked up, Kenyon was on the other side of the car, bent so his head was inside of it as he buckled Austin in.

She couldn't read the look on his face as he gazed at her, but it seemed the interaction between her and Beacon had affected him.

Austin, who had been sucking on two of his fingers, popped them out of his mouth and pointed at his father. "Love you, Daddy."

"Love you too, buddy." His voice had a faraway quality.

Raina got into the passenger seat while Kenyon climbed behind the wheel. After starting the car and pulling out of the parking space, Kenyon spoke in a soft voice as if he was thinking about something. "I'll stay with you guys for as long as I can. Wish it could be all night."

"Trish will be on guard duty through the night and I'm sure the PCPD will send a patrol by."

"I just wish it was me though," said Kenyon.

His comment held an air of mystery. She wasn't sure what was going on in his mind.

Trisha followed behind Kenyon's car as they wove through city streets.

Kenyon slowed down as he came to a white house with tan trim. "This is it."

He pulled into the driveway by the garage, and Trish parked on the street. Once she got out of her vehicle, Trish put her hands on her hips and stared at the house. "Hard to believe that six months ago I was in this same safe house with Gabe."

Trish's life had been under threat by a man who was searching for a key that her now deceased ex-husband had hidden in her house. The key was to a safety deposit box that held gold her ex had stolen.

Raina looked at the blackened bushes and trees around the house where the man looking for the key had set a fire in an effort to smoke Trisha out.

Once the boys were out of their car seats, they entered the house. Trish took the boys by the hands. "If I remember correctly, one of these rooms has a rather large toy box."

Both the boys clapped their hands. Trish led them to a room with a backward eyebrow raised glance at Raina. A signal between sisters. Trisha was indicating she was taking the boys so she and Kenyon could have some time alone.

Raina lifted her head at the sound of the boys running around and making gleeful noises. "They're having fun." When she turned toward him, Kenyon was standing very close to her. The look in his blue eyes was magnetic.

"I don't want to see you hurt again. I don't know what I'd do without you."

His voice held an intensity she hadn't heard before.

He took her in his arms, pulled her close and kissed her.

Raina stepped back in shock. Her heart beat out of control, and she still felt like she was melting from the warmth of his touch. "Where did that come from?"

He shook his head and began to pace. "I'm not sure. Now I've gone and made everything so awkward."

I'm not sure was hardly a declaration of love or affection.

"I'm sorry. So sorry." Kenyon escaped to the kitchen, still shaking his head. The kitchen door closed but remained ajar.

She brought her fingertips up to her mouth. She'd dreamed of that kiss since she was nineteen, but somehow, she'd imagined that it would be different, that the warm blissful moment would last longer and that it would be clear confirmation that Kenyon felt the same way about her as she did about him.

Peanut let out a little whine. Chewy imitated the same noise.

"My feelings exactly." Raina stared down at the female beagle and her smaller counterpart.

Now they really needed to talk. She stepped toward the door, but the sound of both boys thundering back into the living room gave her pause.

"Look what I found." Austin held up a wooden airplane.

"I found this." Beacon ran ahead of his brother. He held a stuffed horse.

She could hear Kenyon's voice behind her as he came through the kitchen door. "Hey, guys, looks like you have some fun toys."

"There's more in the toy box. Wanna see?" Austin grabbed his Dad's hand.

"Sure," said Kenyon.

The boy led him toward the bedroom as Trisha entered the living room.

Beacon glanced over his shoulder. "Come on, Raina."

"I'll be there."

Trisha stepped toward her sister, brow furrowed. "Everything okay? You look like you just got off the Tilt-A-Whirl."

Raina laughed. What a funny way to put it. Did she look like she'd just been on a scary gravity-defying ride? "You're not going to believe what just happened."

"Try me."

"Kenyon kissed me."

"You say that like it's a bad thing," said Trish.

"I think it was impulsive, and he regretted it seconds after it happened. Honestly, I don't know what is going on in that man's head anymore."

Beacon came into the kitchen. "Raina, come on. There's a game we can play." He held up his fingers with his thumb bent toward his palm. "It takes this many to play."

Raina followed Beacon into the bedroom, which had been set up for kids. Two twin beds, some books and a toy box.

Kenyon and Austin had already spread a board out on the kid-sized table. As they rolled dice and moved their pawns around the table, she caught Kenyon's nervous glances.

The rest of the evening involved both working together to entertain and feed the twins. Kenyon seemed to engineer things so they were not alone together for the rest of the night, even when Trisha offered to give him a break. They worked so well together as co-parents, why couldn't things come together in the romance department?

While they were sitting on the couch eating popcorn and watching a kid's movie, Kenyon's phone rang.

He stared at it. "I got to take this."

He wandered into the next room.

"Is Daddy going away?" Austin spoke as he munched on popcorn.

"Yes, probably." Raina wrapped her arms around both boys and drew them close. "I'm staying here. You won't be able to get rid of me."

"Forever and ever, Raina." Beacon tilted his head.

The look on his face made it feel like she'd been punched in the chest, taking her breath away. "I'll do my best."

Beacon whirled around in his seat and stared at the cartoons flashing on the TV screen. "I want forever and ever."

The images from the screen danced in his eyes as a sadness spread through her. She didn't want to make a promise she wasn't sure she could keep. "Only God knows the future, Beacon." Forever and ever would be nice.

Beacon patted her hand. "Yes, and we have to trust Him."

The wisdom of children never ceased to amaze her. She kissed the top of his head. "So true."

Kenyon emerged from the kitchen. "That was Daniel. We're going to do that thing I talked to you about earlier."

"What thing?" Austin didn't take his eyes off the TV.

"Just something I need to take care of, son."

"You'll come back to our new house," said Beacon.

That was how Beacon had rationalized all the changes in his mind.

Kenyon moved toward the couch. "Not only will I come back, but I'll tickle you and toss you in the air." He swept Beacon up, turned in a circle and then swung him back and forth until the boy laughed.

Austin slipped off the couch with his arms in the air. "Me next, Daddy. Me next."

Kenyon put Beacon down and picked Austin up, putting his arm under his belly. "You're an airplane."

He flew Austin around the room while he made airplane noises and Austin laughed. He put Austin down, and the boys ran back in the bedroom to play. Trish had made herself scarce as well.

Raina stood several feet away from Kenyon as he moved toward the door. She'd never felt uncomfortable around Kenyon, but the kiss had changed all that.

While one hand was already on the doorknob, Kenyon gave her an awkward wave. "Well, see ya." He pulled open the door with Peanut heeling beside him.

She did not step toward him. A hug would just be inviting more confusion into their relationship at this point. "Hope you're successful tonight. Maybe we can get back to…normal."

What was normal for them anyway? She couldn't say. "Lock this after I leave."

He stepped outside, shutting the door behind him. She moved toward the door and locked it. From the window beside the door, she watched Kenyon load Peanut and get in his car and drive away, feeling a sadness that was almost unbearable.

Maybe the kiss had been a blessing in disguise. Evidence that taking their relationship to another level would only ruin what they had had together for so many years.

She turned and stared at the empty living room while the laughter and noise of Trish interacting with the boys in the other bedroom permeated her awareness.

She prayed that Kenyon and the team would be successful tonight, so the twins would once again be safe, even if her future with them was uncertain.

God, please bring Kenyon home safely. Help him catch that woman and the man who is helping her.

The only thing she knew for sure about her life right now was that with Tanya Starling, they were dealing with a very dangerous woman.

TEN

With Peanut close by, Kenyon placed one of the child-sized dummies underneath the covers where Beacon usually slept while Daniel did the same for the bed where Austin should be sleeping.

Daniel turned the dummy's head to the side and pulled the covers up past the shoulders. "Does it look convincing?"

Kenyon nodded. "In the dark. I think she'll be fooled long enough for us to nab her." He drew his attention to the broken window that was still just covered with tape. The door was locked, so Tanya might try to come in through the window. In order to get her on attempted kidnapping charges, they would have to wait until she was in the house and by Beacon's bed. Catching her in the yard would only result in criminal trespass at best. Even though he could identify Tanya, Beacon was so young that his testimony might be questioned. An attempted kidnapping charge where she was caught in the act would ensure she'd be put away for a long time.

Daniel stared at the dummy, adjusting the blanket and then touching the head.

He must be thinking about the child in his own life. "How are things going with Joy?"

"Serena's not doing so good. It won't be long now." His

voice filled with sorrow. "Then I guess I become a father to Joy. Her sole parent."

"I remember when Monique was pregnant with the twins. I was so afraid that I wouldn't know what I was doing."

"What did you find out after they were born?"

"I discovered that, yes, I did make mistakes, but it didn't matter. I can't tell you what it was like the day they were born. I just didn't expect that kind of love to flow through me." He was so grateful for having gotten that specific memory back. The neurologist had shown him a photograph of Monique holding the twins in the hospital. The memory had come rushing back in such a powerful way that he'd cried.

"Joy already has had a rough start. What if I make everything worse for her?"

Kenyon gave Daniel a friendly punch in the shoulder. "You'll do just fine. You've already made a commitment that you are going to take care of her after Serena passes. After that, it's just about love and showing up."

Daniel nodded but didn't say anything right away, as if he were thinking about what Kenyon said. "I hope that's true. I'll be a single dad, a whole new world for me."

Zach's voice came through the radio. "I'm in place just up the street with a view of the front of the house."

"Copy that," said Kenyon. "Jenna, where are you?"

"I just pulled up and have visual on the back side of the house."

The task force members in the two civilian cars outside would alert Daniel and Kenyon to any suspicious presence on either side of the house, so they would be ready. He was glad the other members of the DGTF had offered to help.

Though he was a latecomer to the task force, it made him feel like he belonged.

Both Raina's and Kenyon's cars were parked in the driveway. Lights had been left on in the kitchen making it look like someone was home, but the rest of the lights were turned off, so Tanya would assume everyone had gone to bed.

"Let's get this done," said Kenyon. He moved toward the open closet and sat down behind the door, pushed back out of view. Peanut slipped in beside him. Daniel took up his place on the far side of Austin's bed by the interior door. Daniel had brought his partner, Great Dane Dakota, along but left her in the room across the hall with the door open. Her size made it impossible to hide her. Because she was trained in protection, she might be needed. She'd get to the room with a single one-word command.

A night-light illuminated the boys' beds, but not enough to give away that the bodies underneath the blankets were not human.

Kenyon spoke into the radio. "We're in position."

Kenyon pressed his back against the wall of the closet. Something hard and uncomfortable pushed against his bottom. He shifted slightly and felt metal. One of Austin's little cars.

After getting comfortable, he settled in, hearing only a slight rustling as Daniel found a position he could maintain for hours. Now began the hard part of a stakeout, the waiting. His mind wandered from thinking about the gun trafficking investigation to Raina and the kiss.

Why had he done something so foolish and impulsive? Part of it was because he'd almost died in that explosion. But then when they'd been getting the boys out of their car seats, he'd been so deeply moved by watching how Raina interacted with Beacon. The love and connection she had with both boys drew him to her. The more time he spent with her especially when they were taking care of the twins together, the stronger the feelings became.

When he'd been wandering not knowing who he was. He would see children in a park and feel a physical pain in his chest but not know why. The whole time, he had no clear memory of the twins, what they looked like, only intense longing when he was around children. The longing had at one point even led him back to this house, though cognitively he didn't know it was his house. The heart finds its way back even if the head doesn't cooperate. Now maybe his heart was telling him something about Raina that his head refused to hear.

He leaned against the wall of the closet and stared at the ceiling.

At least an hour went by as the two men waited in the bedroom. Kenyon blinked and shook his head in an effort to stay awake. It was so quiet in the house he could hear Daniel shift around.

Then Kenyon's radio crackled. "Suspicious activity about a block away. Looks to be a female making her way up the sidewalk alone. Dressed in black." The voice was Zach's. He was parked with a view of the front of the house.

"Her partner must be waiting in the getaway car for her out of sight." Daniel spoke into his radio in a low voice.

"She's headed up your walkway," Zach announced.

Kenyon tensed knowing Tanya was so close. This was it.

"Looked in the window. Now she's at the front door. Can't see clearly, but she must have some kind of lock pick kit."

So she wasn't going to try to get in through the bedroom window. The soft thud from the bedroom told him Daniel was changing his position. If she came through the door that connected to the hallway, he'd be spotted. He must have moved closer to Beacon's bed by the window to stay hidden.

"She's in," whispered Zach.

Kenyon took in a deep breath. Adrenaline pumped through his body, but he remained still. Peanut's motionless body pressed against his side. Outside the closed bedroom door, he heard what might be footsteps, but the noise never got louder. She must be looking around. He could discern only the slightest rustling, and it wasn't clear what part of the house she was in.

Without having to say anything, all the officers knew they needed to have radio silence.

Maybe she was figuring out that this was a setup. They had to wait. If they moved on her now, they could charge her with breaking and entering. She'd be out on bail fairly quickly.

Kenyon let out a slow breath and pressed his back against the wall.

The silence enveloped him. His heartbeat pulsed in his ears. What was she doing?

Was she looking in the other rooms? If she found Raina's and Kenyon's bedrooms empty, she'd know she was being set up.

If that was the case, she'd run. He scooted forward in the closet.

Jenna's low voice came through the radio. "Someone just jumped the fence into your backyard."

Tanya's accomplice. Jenna had had a good reason to break radio silence. It looked like the plan was to hand Beacon through the window to the accomplice after Tanya broke in through the front door.

He waited for the sound of the bedroom door creaking

open, but it never came. He thought he heard a low voice somewhere in the house, but he couldn't be sure.

"Something's up. He's back over the fence."

Tanya had figured out she'd been set up. Kenyon burst to his feet and headed toward the door with Peanut beside him. Daniel was already crawling through the window in pursuit of the accomplice. Kenyon swung open the door. Tanya had to still be in the house or Zach would have let him know.

He could not see Tanya, but he could hear her retreating footsteps. When he got to the living room, the front door was open.

"She's out," said Zach.

Kenyon hurried outside, the porch light providing only a little illumination. He saw no sign of their target.

"Hard to see. Think she's headed south up Grand Street. Will pursue by car," said Zach.

Kenyon ran faster toward where Tanya had fled.

The lights of the unmarked police car were behind him. The padding of rapid footsteps on the concrete sidewalk ended. Tanya had cut away from the street.

"Will pursue on foot." Kenyon spoke into his radio.

"Roger that. I'll circle the block. She's got to come out somewhere."

With Peanut by his side, Kenyon darted down an alley. Up ahead, a dog barked from behind a fence. He moved toward the sound, assuming it was Tanya running by that had alarmed the dog. The alley led to a park. He scanned the area looking for movement. Tanya was dressed in dark colors and hard to see. Blown by the wind, some of the playground equipment creaked.

He pulled his flashlight, searching but not seeing any sign of Tanya. After alerting Zach to where he was, he strode toward a tower connected to a slide where some-one might hide.

Peanut alerted by sitting down. Someone with a gun was close by.

A second later, a gunshot shattered the silence. He hit the ground on his stomach before another shot filled the air. Peanut pressed close to him. The shots had come from behind him. After putting his flashlight back in his belt, he crawled toward the shelter of the tower and searched where he thought the shot had come from at the periphery of the park. Had she fired and taken off or was she hop-ing to get another chance to take him out? Though he saw no sign of Tanya, she could be hiding behind some of the playground equipment.

He pulled his own weapon, running the short distance to where he thought the shot had come from and taking cover behind various pieces of playground equipment with Peanut by his side. Another shot whizzed past him as he ducked be-hind a playhouse. He fired back, guessing at where she was.

He tuned his ears to the sounds around him. The swings creaked in the nighttime breeze. Wind rustled the nearly bare tree branches.

Once again, he pulled his flashlight and swung it in an arc around the park. A light color flashed and was gone. Tanya's face maybe. He sprinted in the direction he thought she'd gone running, past several houses and then into a grove of trees.

Aware that she could be hiding in the trees, he slowed as he held his weapon, stepping off the path that led through the grove. Though he braced for another gunshot, none came. He stepped out onto a path that ran past the back side of several houses. He was out of breath from running.

"Anything?" Zach sounded staticky on the radio.

"I think I lost her." He could not hide the note of defeat in his voice.

"What street are you close to? I'll swing around and pick you up."

"Give me a second." He could see a streetlamp on the other side of the houses that bordered the grove of trees. He jogged in that direction.

When he stepped out onto the street, he saw the headlights of Zach's car several blocks away.

"I see you," said Zach.

The cab of Zach's vehicle was warm inside when he loaded Peanut into the front seat, holding her in his lap.

Daniel's voice came through the radio. "Looks like the accomplice got away. No sign of him here. We've been up and down the streets around the house."

"Thanks, Daniel," said Zach.

As if understanding how disappointing the situation was, Peanut licked Kenyon's hand. Kenyon stroked the dog's head.

"Let's debrief at headquarters, and then we'll all go home and get some sleep," said Daniel.

"Copy that," said Jenna.

Tension threaded through Kenyon's chest. Though he was beyond tired, his thoughts raced. They might have to put the twins through identifying the accomplice to move the case forward. The thing that worried him more though was that now Tanya knew they weren't at his house, she would start searching the city for them.

When Raina woke up in her room, she found the police officer who had taken over for Trish dozing in the living room chair beside the window. She checked Kenyon's room. The bed had not been slept in.

Worried thoughts filled her mind as she returned to the living room.

The officer opened his eyes.

"Did Kenyon come home?" The lilt in her voice gave away the fear she was experiencing.

"Yeah, he came in a while ago. Went to sleep in the room with his kids."

Raina eased the door open to the room where the boys were staying. Chewy lay at the end of Austin's bed and Kenyon held Beacon in the other twin bed, with Peanut sleeping on the floor beside them. Such a picture of serenity.

She closed the door softly and retreated to the kitchen to make coffee. When she turned around, Kenyon was in the doorway. She set the cup of coffee she'd just poured for herself on the counter.

"Sorry, I hope I didn't wake you."

He shook his head. Though he'd taken off his jacket, he was still in his clothes. His shirt was untucked, and his hair was messy. It looked as if he had had a long night.

"I've got some coffee started here." She opened a cupboard and reached for another mug. After pouring the hot brew, she handed the cup to him. "So how did it go last night?"

His disheveled appearance and the level of fatigue she saw in his expression all hinted that the sting had not worked. It seemed like it would have been the first thing he'd told her if it had gone well.

"We didn't catch them."

"You look so tired. Why don't you sit down, and I'll fix you some breakfast?"

"Thank you." His hand brushed over her bare arm, causing a surge of warmth that reached her cheeks. The tone of appreciation in his voice made her heart flutter.

She pulled eggs and butter from the refrigerator and proceeded to fry him up some breakfast. "The boys and I made some biscuits last night. I had to do something to keep them busy. Would you like one?"

"Sure, that sounds great."

She placed the eggs and biscuit in front of him along with some jam and butter. He stared down at the biscuit, which was oddly shaped.

He smiled. "Let me guess—you let them form the biscuits by themselves."

"How else will they learn?" She took a sip of her coffee. Already his mood seemed to be lifting.

He stared at the plate. "You're not going to eat?"

"I'm not hungry."

He took a bite of the eggs. "This reminds me of the meals we had a 4-H camp. You remember those."

"Yeah, but we didn't have a nice kitchen then. Cooking over the fire in cast iron, I think everything was a little more burnt."

They both laughed. A flood of memories cycled through her head like snapshots. "That's neat that you remembered that."

They shared a lot of history. All the memories didn't seem to be enough to bind them together in romantic love, though.

When she took a sip of her coffee, it tasted bitter. She grabbed the sugar container and poured some in, stirring it slowly. "Do you think the boys and I are safe here?"

Kenyon nodded. "No place is going to be totally safe, but this is the most secure place the department can provide with the highest level of protection. The windows are bulletproof glass. You have to have a key code to get inside."

Both of them were choosing not to talk about the kiss.

The best thing to do would be to go back to the status quo. She was his best friend. She was helping take care of two boys she'd come to love.

"So what's the next step? How are you going to catch Tanya?"

"She hasn't been returning to her house. She must be hiding out somewhere in Plains City. It would help if we could identify her accomplice."

"Does that mean you'll want to question the boys about what they saw when he tried to come through their window?"

Kenyon nodded. "I didn't want to put them through that, but it might be the only thing that moves the case forward."

She had overheard the boys talking to each other about what had happened to them. Each vowing to protect the other if it happened again. "I do think they saw him. They kept calling him the earring man."

"That's a pretty distinct detail." Kenyon finished his last bite of breakfast. "Soon as they wake up, I'll talk to them."

She checked the clock on the wall. "They should be waking up any minute. I'll have breakfast ready for them."

"I don't want them to be afraid all over again. We need to keep this as low-key as possible. Will you help me?"

The angst she heard in his voice tugged at her heart. Here was a man who had experienced horrible things, and yet his priority was always to protect his sons.

"Sure, of course, Kenyon."

Kenyon left the room to freshen up.

The boys would want to eat the biscuits they'd made for breakfast. She pulled some peanut butter out of the cupboard to add some protein to the meal.

Within the half hour, the boys were up, dressed and

eating biscuits. Raina poured a glass of orange juice for each of them.

Beacon held a stuffed animal while Austin scooted a car across the table in between bites of biscuit.

"This is yummy," said Austin.

Beacon took a gulp of orange juice. "You and me are good bakers, huh, Raina?"

"You sure are."

They only had a few more bites of the meal left. Kenyon returned and locked gazes with Raina for just a moment.

"Guys, do you remember that night at the house when that man tried to get through your window?"

Both boys stopped chewing and nodded.

"The earring man," said Beacon as he stared at the table.

Raina rubbed Beacon's back while Kenyon spoke. "We want to catch this guy."

"And put him in jail?" Austin pushed his car a few inches across the table.

"And put him in jail," said Kenyon.

"We need to know what he looked like."

"Austin saw the earring too." Beacon leaned toward his brother.

"It was big, like a quarter," said Austin.

"And shiny," said Beacon.

At the house, there was a streetlight that illuminated part of the backyard. It sounded like the earring was metal and that light reflected off of it.

"Do you remember anything else about the man?" Raina still rested her hand on Beacon's back. He tugged at the stuffed buffalo's legs and then drew it close to his chest, a sign that he was anxious.

"His hair looked like straw," said Austin.

"No," Beacon swiped Austin's arm with the stuffed animal. "It was orange."

It was possible the limited light could have made it hard to distinguish hair color.

"Anything else, guys?"

Beacon had begun to wiggle in his seat.

"He had on a blue coat," said Austin.

"No, it was black." Beacon's scrunched-up face indicated that he was growing more upset.

Kenyon rose to his feet. "You know what. That's enough of that. Why don't we go play in the room for a while? We can build a fort."

The boys slipped off their chairs, making happy sounds. Kenyon and Austin stepped into the living room. Beacon looked back at Raina. "Are you coming too?"

"I'll be there in just a minute."

Beacon ran out of the kitchen.

Raina picked up the empty plates and cups and put them in the sink. She was glad Kenyon had ended the questions before Beacon got too agitated.

When she turned back around, Kenyon had stuck his head in the kitchen. She could hear the boys shouting and jumping around in their temporary bedroom.

"I gotta get to work."

"Really, after that long night?" There was a desperate pleading quality to her voice that she had not experienced before.

He gathered her into his arms. "I'll get back as fast as I can."

She felt herself melting against him. This was more than just the friendly hugs they used to share. She needed him now more than she ever had. They needed each other to get through this.

They both pulled free of the hug almost as quickly as they'd fallen into it. She turned back toward the sink and scrubbed one of the plates with a little too much vigor. Yet another awkward moment for the record books.

"I'm going to phone Cheyenne on the drive over with the information about the earring and that his hair might be an unusual color, yellow or orange. Maybe it will turn up something."

She nodded without turning to face him, fearing that she would fall apart if she did. She listened to his retreating footsteps. Still holding the now clean plate, she closed her eyes when he said goodbye to the boys. She waited for the sound of the door opening and closing but didn't hear it.

When she turned around, Kenyon was standing in the doorway. "I'll check if I can go into work later so I can stay here with you and the boys a little longer."

Tears filled her eyes. "Thank you." He did understand that the burden of caring for the boys under such trying circumstances was too much for her to bear alone.

They stood feet apart. No need to experience another awkward hug.

"I still need to phone Cheyenne and see if she can get started on figuring out who Tanya's accomplice is."

"It's not much to go on."

"Cheyenne is pretty good at putting puzzles together, even when she doesn't have all the pieces," said Kenyon.

It was clear that, except for the earring, the boys' memory of the man differed slightly. Would that information be enough for them to find Tanya's accomplice? Would finding out who he was get them any closer to catching Tanya?

ELEVEN

Hours later, as he stepped into the kitchen to take the incoming call from Cheyenne, Kenyon felt restless and conflicted. He wanted to take down the men who had been responsible for so much destruction and personal trials. But he also found himself not wanting to leave Raina and the boys.

Kenyon and Raina had played pirates with the boys through the morning until they were ready to go down for a nap. It had taken only a quick phone call to Daniel for him to get the morning off, and then he'd made another call to Cheyenne.

He pressed the connect button. "Tell me something good."

"I think I might know who our earring guy is."

"How did you manage that?"

"The interviews with the neighbors indicated Tanya was heavily into martial arts. So I tracked down some photos from the dojo she's a member of in the town where she lives."

"Let me guess. Earring guy is in the picture."

"An earring like a coin and hair that is either yellow or orange is not much to go on, but there is a guy in the photograph who matches that description."

"We have a name for him I assume?"

"Yes, Vernon Cunningham. It gets better than that. He owns the dojo where Tanya trains and several others across the state. One of which is in Plains City."

"What do you want to bet that is where Tanya is hiding out? What's the name of the dojo?"

"Powerhouse Academy on Lincoln Street. I already told Daniel about what I found. West will be available to help you check it out within the hour. He'll meet you at the station house."

"Perfect. Thanks, Cheyenne," said Kenyon.

"One final thing. I'm in the process of enlarging and cropping the photo of Vernon. I should have it sent to yours and West's phones before you get to the station house."

"You think of everything. Thanks again." He pressed the disconnect button.

Kenyon found Raina in her room sitting in a chair reading a book. She looked up at him, green eyes filled with light. "Good news?"

She knew him so well she could read his expressions like a book. "We got a lead on the accomplice and a possible hiding place for Tanya. It means I need to go and check it out."

"I understand. Thank you for staying the morning with us. That meant a lot to me."

When she'd looked at him with tears in her eyes in the kitchen, he'd realized how much of a burden she carried over keeping the boys safe. She'd given up so much and demanded so little. It was beyond unfair for her to bear the weight of caring for his sons under these circumstances.

"The sooner we get her in custody, the sooner we can get back to normal."

"And what is normal for us, Kenyon?" Her expression was without guile, and her voice held no tone of accusation.

She had been so patient. He needed to start thinking about what was best for her too. He couldn't keep her in limbo while he tried to figure out his feelings. Hadn't she already given up enough to help him?

"You deserve a life of your own. I'll understand when this is all over if you need to move back to your own house."

Her jaw dropped. "But… I'll still help out with the twins."

"I want you in the twins' lives as much as possible, but it's unfair to keep you hanging in such a place of uncertainty." He could feel his chest growing tighter as he spoke. The words were hard to say, but he knew it was wrong to rob her of a future. "I've been really selfish."

"My moving out could be really disruptive for Austin and Beacon," she said.

It touched him so deeply that her foremost concern was toward his sons. "Yes, we need to talk through the best way to make the transition as smoothly as possible for them."

"I guess, we'll work it out when we have to." Her voice had grown even softer.

He thought he read distress in her eyes. Through no choice of their own, this whole thing was such a tangled mess. There was no easy way to untangle it.

"Yes. We'll figure it out together, but first let's end this nightmare that Tanya has put us in." He left the room and hurried toward the door.

On the drive across town, Raina's face and the softness of her voice kept flashing through his mind. He'd enjoyed playing with his sons. The morning had turned out to be a sweet escape from all he'd been dealing with. It was getting harder each time to leave those three.

Telling Raina it would be okay for her to move out had not been easy. But it was the right thing to do. Was his attraction just about the way she cared for and loved his sons or was there something deeper there? He wasn't sure.

When he arrived at the PCPD parking lot, West was already waiting for him in his car with Gus in the kennel in the back.

Kenyon exited his car and approached West, who rolled down the window when Kenyon got close. "I'm going to grab that baseball hat out of evidence. Even if Tanya isn't at the dojo right now, the dogs will alert if she has been there recently."

"Good idea," said West.

Kenyon hurried inside and checked the hat out from the evidence clerk. The dojo was not far from the station house. They pulled into a parking lot where there were several other cars. None of them looked like the one he'd seen on the street watching his house.

The dojo had floor-to-ceiling windows. Kenyon could see that there was a class taking place inside. Six kids in *gis* warmed up, mirroring the moves of their male instructor. He glanced at the photo that Cheyenne had sent him. The instructor looked nothing like Vernon, too old and too heavy through the middle. Vernon appeared to be in top-notch condition.

West looked at him. "How do you want this to go down?"

Kenyon peered through the windows again. It was a two-story building. There were probably offices upstairs where Vernon or Tanya might be. He could see several doors behind the instruction area that might be for equipment storage.

"Let's just go inside and ask permission to let the dogs have a look around."

They deployed the dogs and stepped inside. The instructor walked over to them after telling the students, who all looked to be under ten years of age, to do a drill. The kids moved through the drill half-heartedly, placing their attention on the dogs.

The instructor came toward them. "Can I help you?"

"We think that someone involved in a crime may have been in this building. We'd like to let the K-9s have a look around."

"I guess that would be okay. The manager is not here right now."

"Have you seen the owner of the dojo, Vernon Cunningham, lately?"

"Yes, he's been around."

"Have you seen a new woman around here, say in the last few days, slender, brown hair? She's a martial artist as well."

The instructor shook his head. "Can't say as I have. No one new that I've noticed. I only teach three classes a week."

"Thank you for letting us have a look around," said Kenyon.

West put the hat under Gus's nose. The dog did several circles through the training area before heading up the stairs.

Kenyon remained on the first floor. Tanya had at least one gun. Peanut would be able to tell him if any firearms had been in the building. "Pea, find tools."

The dog put her nose to the ground. After running in a circle and then toward a pile of mats and sniffing it, Peanut headed toward a door on the far side of the instruction area. She sat back and stared at the door, a solid alert. When he tried the door, it was locked.

West had disappeared up the stairs with Gus.

Kenyon signaled to the instructor, who was watching the kids spar. The instructor walked over to Kenyon.

"My dog seems to think there's a firearm in here. What is this closet used for?"

"That's not a storage closet we access much. The newer equipment is kept over there." He pointed to a wall where there was another door.

"Can we have a look inside here?" Peanut continued to stare intensely at the door.

The instructor shook his head. "I should be clearing this with the manager."

"The crime we're investigating involves the kidnapping of a child," said Kenyon.

That information seemed to help the instructor make his decision.

He pulled a set of keys from his pocket. Peanut rushed into the room, sniffing the lower shelves and then getting on her hind feet until she alerted. Kenyon moved in and lifted the box of sparring gloves that Peanut had indicated. Behind the box at the back of the shelf was a gun.

"Good girl, Pea." Kenyon pulled the ducky out of his pocket for Peanut to play with to reward her for her good work.

He picked the gun and placed it in the evidence bag he had with him.

Kenyon's radio crackled as West's voice came across the line. "Gus followed a scent up to the roof. Looks like we have a sort of makeshift camp up here. A tent and a cot and a battery-powered heater. There's an exterior stairs that she could have come and gone by without being noticed."

"That probably means that she's been staying here. Kind

of cold to be sleeping outside in October. Is there anything to indicate the sleeping quarters belong to Tanya?"

"Let me check." The noise of shuffling and moving things around came through the radio. "Bingo. I got an old photo here of Tanya with her mom and dad and Joey."

"We found a gun down here that I'm sure will prove to be hers. We'll have to put this place under surveillance."

Kenyon stepped out of the closet. His attention was drawn to the front door.

Though his hair was more red than orange, Vernon Cunningham stood just inside the dojo.

Shock spread across Vernon's face then he turned and ran out the door.

Kenyon hadn't even had time to lift his finger from the talk button on the radio. "Vernon's here. I'm in pursuit."

With Peanut by his side, Kenyon stepped out into the parking lot in time to see Vernon jump in his car and speed up the street.

Kenyon didn't take the time to load Peanut in her kennel. Instead he commanded her to jump into the front seat. She moved over to the passenger side. Kenyon tossed the gun in the evidence bag and started his car.

He radioed West. "Headed east up Lincoln Street."

"We're right behind you."

Vernon wove through downtown traffic. He turned into a mall parking lot.

Kenyon scanned the whole area, not seeing the car. "I'm at the Black Hills Mall. I've lost him."

"I'm about three minutes away," came West's reply.

Kenyon circled around several rows of cars until he spotted the car Vernon had been driving. It was partially concealed by two large trucks on both sides of it.

Peanut made a yipping noise and wiggled in the passenger seat.

"Approaching the vehicle just outside of Big Dan's Sporting Goods." Kenyon stopped his car and jumped out with his gun drawn. He caught a glimpse of West's car turning into the lot and headed toward him.

He stepped toward Vernon's car and peered in. Empty. He turned his head toward his shoulder mike. "I think he's gone inside."

West parked by the curb that bordered the sporting goods store. He deployed Gus and disappeared inside.

Kenyon took a separate entrance next to the sporting goods place. Peanut heeled by his side. He stepped into a wide corridor that provided a view of quite a few shops. The place was bustling with activity. The guy could be hiding in a restroom or nestled in the back of the one of the many stores.

Vernon had been wearing a lime green shirt. Kenyon walked the corridor, focusing in on that color.

"I could search this store all day." Even over the radio West sounded like he was out of breath and running. "He's not in the restroom in here."

"Keep looking. I wasn't that far behind him. He's got on a lime green shirt that's almost neon. His hair is an unnatural shade of red." Kenyon peered into a bookstore as he walked past. The next store he trotted past was a very open jewelry store that would provide no place to hide. He kept scanning as he stepped through a cluster of teenage girls.

Green flashed in his peripheral vision. Kenyon pivoted to see a man moving toward an exit. Not running but moving at a brisk walk. He sprinted to get a closer look. He saw the man from the back. He had Vernon's muscular build and reddish hair.

Kenyon took off running. "Got him. Headed out by the Almost Mom's café exit."

Kenyon burst into an all-out run. Peanut kept pace with him. Once outside, his gaze bounced toward where Vernon had parked his car. Sure enough, the perp was headed in that direction. Kenyon sprinted, weaving between cars to cut Vernon off.

Kenyon closed the distance between himself and the other man. "Stop police."

Vernon stopped, turned and delivered a roundhouse kick to Kenyon's chest area. The move took the wind out of him, but he remained upright. Vernon landed a blow to Kenyon's face before turning and running.

"Hey!" Vernon let out a cry as Peanut sunk her teeth into his pant leg. He tried to keep running, but the weight of the little beagle slowed him down.

Kenyon caught up to him and grabbed him by the back of the shoulders. "Police. You're under arrest."

"For what?" Vernon's voice lacked defiance.

"For aiding in an attempted kidnapping." Peanut sat at attention, her nose in the air. "Good work, Sweet Pea." He tossed the squeaky ducky so Peanut could get her reward for being such a great partner.

Kenyon pulled his cuffs.

Vernon hung his head. "I was only trying to help a friend."

Kenyon slapped the cuffs on Vernon. "What did she tell you?"

"The kid was hers. He was taken from her and adopted illegally. She had him when she was a teenager. She's been looking for him for almost four years. Tanya's had so many rough breaks. I wanted to help her out."

"That was some sob story she'd created. None of that is true."

"Really?"

Vernon sounded genuinely surprised. Tanya had deceived him in order to get his assistance and a place to stay.

Kenyon wondered if Vernon knew that Beacon was a twin, then realized he had his answer. The guy must not have seen both boys when he looked through the window. If he had, he would have known that Tanya's story about having her child taken from her was fabricated.

"How many guns does she have?"

"At least three that I know of."

Assuming the gun they found at the dojo was hers, that meant she still had two. "Where is she now?"

"I don't know. She hasn't been back to the dojo. After the stunt you guys pulled last night trying to set her up, she went ballistic. I've never seen her so angry."

West came up to Kenyon and Vernon. "I'll bring the car by so we can take him in." He ran off, with Gus following him.

Kenyon spun Vernon around. "So you have no idea where she is?"

Vernon shook his head. "She's always been a little bit of a hothead. I tried to help her to channel her rage into her training. I have to tell you. Some of the things she said were scary. She's especially angry at the kid's adoptive mother."

"She's not the kid's mom, adoptive or otherwise. Tanya lied to you."

"Okay, well, Tanya's out for blood."

Kenyon's chest tightened with fear for Raina. "What do you mean?"

"Tanya views the redhead as being in the way. She wants her dead."

TWELVE

Raina was grateful when she saw her sister headed up the walkway to the safe house. The boys were playing quietly in their room. Trish was here as part of the protection duty, but having her sister close would give her a chance to talk to someone about what Kenyon had said to her about moving out once Tanya was caught.

All day long, she'd been thinking about what he'd said. His decision had devastated her. Yet, he'd kept his word and given her an answer about what the future would look like for all of them. Kenyon had implied that he'd been unkind to keep her hanging on. Maybe she did need to let go of the idea that they would be a couple. She knew you couldn't make someone fall in love with you.

It was just that the kiss confused her.

The police officer rose to his feet to unlock the door for Trish. He patted Trisha's shoulder as she stepped inside before waving at Raina.

"See you, Raina. Take care," he said, then stepped outside.

The sky had already begun to grow gray as the two women watched through the window while the police officer walked toward the unmarked police car.

She'd seen a police car drive by earlier, and she was sure

that one would patrol the neighborhood at least one or two more times before night fell.

"Everything been quiet here?" Trish turned toward her sister.

"In terms of feeling like this is a safe place, yes."

The boys came running out of their room with Chewy trailing behind as they yelled Trish's name and jumped up and down.

"We've been building things," said Austin.

Beacon grabbed Trish's free hand. "Wanna see?"

"Sure." As the boys led her toward their room, she gave a backward glance toward Raina. The raised eyebrows communicated that she knew Raina wanted to talk. She was confident they'd find some time while Trish was on duty.

"I'll get started on dinner," said Raina.

Before she could make it to the kitchen, she heard a light knocking on the door. She moved toward the window. She noticed that the police officer who just left had forgotten his book on the table by the chair that gave him a view of the street. Maybe he was coming back for it.

When she peered out the window by the door, there were two kids standing on her small porch. One carried boxes of cookies and the other held what looked to be a catalogue. They were probably trying to raise money for some school thing.

This was a neighborhood, and most of the people probably thought this house was some sort of vacation rental or a second home for someone. She didn't want to raise alarm bells by not answering the door.

As a precaution, she called out to her sister.

When she opened the door, the kids were already running up the block. She stood staring up and down the street.

The hair on her neck prickled. She slammed the door shut and clicked both locks.

Trish had come back in the living room with the boys trailing behind her. "Everything all right? Did you open that door?"

"There were some kids selling things. They saw me through the front window. I thought it would look weird if I didn't answer the door."

"I suppose so," said Trish.

She remembered that Trish had told her that the glass in the windows was bulletproof. The only way someone could take a shot at her was if she was standing out in the open. Yet, no shot had been fired.

Both of them looked at the twins. Now was not the time to talk about potential dangers.

"I'll just get dinner started." Raina headed back toward the kitchen.

Trish held her hand out to the boys. "Come on, guys. Let's go back in the bedroom."

Raina pulled hamburger and sausage out of the fridge to brown for spaghetti. She got the other ingredients out of the cupboards and set them on the counter.

The kitchen window looked out on several houses that were in various stages of being built. The two children she'd seen earlier were standing on a concrete foundation with only the exterior frame of the house up.

They no longer held the boxes of cookies or the catalogue. They were standing close together as one placed something in the other's open hand. The older girl was counting out money for the younger one. They both looked in Raina's direction, guilt written on their faces, and then they ran toward the cover of a house that had the siding on it.

Raina's heart beat a little faster as she refocused to look through the kitchen window, noticing there was a pucker in the glass and what looked like a bullet embedded there. That had to have happened earlier in the day.

She pivoted so quickly she knocked a can of tomatoes on the floor. "Trish."

She moved toward the living room saying Trish's name again. She could hear Trish quieting the boys before she emerged alone from the bedroom.

"What is it?"

She grabbed her sister's hand. "She knows we're here."

"How? What are you talking about?"

She pulled Trish into the kitchen and pointed at the embedded bullet.

Trisha's shoulders touched her ears. Her voice was icy. "Oh my. Did you actually see Tanya?"

"No, but I saw those two kids who came to the door out back counting money...like they'd been paid to lure me out of the house."

"Why would Tanya do that?"

"To make sure it was me and therefore Beacon inside." Raina shuddered. "Or to have a clean shot at me when I stepped out on the porch since the earlier bullet didn't work."

Trish pulled her gun. "You stay here inside with Austin and Beacon. I'll do a patrol around the house. Lock the door behind me. I can use the code to get back in."

Raina locked the kitchen door after Trish stepped out. She watched her sister through the window as she moved toward the house under construction and then around to the front of the house. Trish came back through the front door.

"Anything?"

"Not that I could see. All the cars on the street with a

view of this place are unoccupied. I suppose there are other places someone could watch the house from."

"Trish, I just don't want to take any chances."

"I understand. I'd do the same thing if I felt in my gut Gabriel was unsafe." Trish nodded. "I'll have to clear a move with Captain Ross. I'm not sure what our options are."

"Thank you. I don't feel like we can waste any time. We have to get out of here." Raina was already running back toward the boys' room.

Trish followed behind her. "We can't do it without some backup. That would just make you and the boys a bigger target."

Raina caught herself. Trish was right. There needed to be a degree of planning if they were to stay safe. Tanya and her accomplice might be watching the house even now. Raina paced outside the twins' room. The door was ajar, and she could hear the sound of their gleeful playing. Their innocent young lives would be disrupted yet again.

Trish had pulled out her phone, which she held against her chest. "I don't even know where we'll go. How do you suppose she found the safe house?"

Raina shook her head. "Maybe she watched the officers leave the station and followed them until one of them led her here."

"Let me call Ross and see what he says." Trish wandered back into the kitchen while she made her phone call.

Raina pulled her own phone out and pressed Kenyon's number.

"Raina." Kenyon sounded out of breath. "I was just getting ready to call you. Everything okay there?"

"I think Tanya has found the safe house."

"What happened? Was anyone hurt?"

"No, we're all safe…for now. I didn't actually see her. It's just that some strange things happened—"

"I'm almost to Lowell Street. We'll get you and the boys out of there and take you to the station until we can find something more permanent."

Kenyon hadn't even asked for details. His voice held a note of fear.

"Kenyon, what's going on?"

"Look, we caught Tanya's accomplice. I'm concerned that Tanya's mental state has become even more volatile. I'm almost there."

Kenyon must have already been on his way back to the safe house to have been so close already.

"I'll get our stuff together," said Raina.

Raina hurried to her room and threw the few items she'd taken out of her suitcase back into it. Kenyon as well had only unpacked his toiletries. When she stepped into the twins' room, Trish was already helping them gather their belongings.

"I called Kenyon. He's on his way. He will escort us to the station for now."

Trish stood up and ushered Raina outside the door. "Ross says there is a second safe house the department owns that might become available in a few days. A witness in a high-profile trial is staying there under protection right now."

"Okay, so we go to the station and figure things out from there."

Trish nodded. They both helped the boys get packed up. As they put their toys and clothes in the duffel, she could see the confused looks on their faces.

"Where are we going now?" Austin slumped across the bed on his stomach.

"We're going to go where your Daddy works. Won't that be fun?"

"I guess." Austin let out a heavy sigh.

By the time they were packed up, she stepped out in the living room just in time to see Kenyon on the porch. He seemed to be hesitating. She ran and opened the door. "Everything okay?"

"It's Peanut. She seems agitated. She didn't do a full alert, but something is bothering her."

Raina put down the suitcase she was carrying. "Tanya could be out there with a gun."

Fear made her want to rush into his arms but she thought better of it. His decision that she should move out seemed to have placed an invisible barrier between them.

Kenyon nodded and then he glanced down at Peanut. "That's a possibility." His voice was faint as though he were thinking about what could have set Peanut on edge.

"The boys are growing tired of all the moves," said Raina.

"Understandable."

Kenyon stood on the threshold of the boys' room.

Trish slipped past Raina. "I'll load the suitcases in my car so you and the boys can ride with Kenyon. I'll follow behind."

She picked up several suitcases and headed out the door.

Light came into Kenyon's eyes. "The car."

Peanut let out a bark of approval.

Kenyon ran toward the now closed door. "Wait Trish!"

"What is it?" Raina followed Kenyon. She'd picked up on the fear in his voice. He swung the door open just as a loud boom surrounded her.

Out the window, she saw an explosive flash and then flames consuming Trish's car.

Raina made her way to the open door. A wall of heat hit her. Fire everywhere. Her knees buckled.

Kenyon caught her, held her up. "Don't go outside." He kicked the door shut with his foot.

"Trisha." The cry for her sister seemed to get caught in her throat.

Was Trish dead?

Please, dear God, no.

Kenyon helped Raina over to a chair. It was clear that she was in shock, unable to speak, eyes glazed.

The boys emerged from the bedroom. "Daddy, what happened?" He glanced out the window to where Trish's car still burned.

"Stay in the house. Go to your room and close the door."

Beacon said, "But Daddy, there's a fire." Beacon's gaze fell on Raina and he ran to her. "Are you okay?"

Raina seemed to shake herself free of her shock. "You heard what Daddy said. Let's go back in the room."

He pressed his radio. "I'm going to need a fire crew and police backup at the safe house on Lowell Street."

With Peanut following him, he stepped out, dreading what he might see. Trish lay face down about five feet from her burning car. She stirred but didn't get up. He spoke into the radio. "And an ambulance."

He rushed over to her. "Trish."

He helped her turn over on her side. She had a cut on her forehead and a smear of dirt across her cheek. She shook her head then stared down at her fisted hand, opening it slowly to reveal her car fob. "I pressed the remote start and then..."

The bomb had been designed to go off when the car started. He glanced around the houses in the neighborhood and at the empty lot. Was Tanya watching to see if her handiwork had been effective? She might have set up another bomb somewhere else since she'd been unable to get in the house in an attempt to lure Raina out.

"Are you all right to stand?"

Trish nodded. Kenyon helped her get to her feet and held her arm until she was inside the house and sitting in a chair. Raina came out of the bedroom and rushed toward her sister. The boys remained in the room.

"Oh, Trish. I'm so glad you're alive." She kneeled and wrapped her arms around her sister.

He couldn't wait for backup. If Tanya was watching, she'd flee once the squad cars arrived. "Help is on the way. Peanut and I need to get back out there."

Kenyon undid the strap that kept his gun in the holster and stepped outside with Peanut by his side. Neighbors had come out on the sidewalk and were peering through second-story windows. He needed to be ready to apprehend Tanya, but he didn't want to scare the innocent bystanders.

He rushed over to an older man and woman who were standing outside the fence of their front yard with their arms wrapped around each other.

"What happened?" said the old man.

"Long story," said Kenyon. "We've got fire crews on the way. Did you notice any strangers in the neighborhood today? Anyone acting suspicious?"

Both of them shook their heads. Kenyon questioned several other onlookers, getting the same answer from each one. Peanut never alerted as they walked the neighborhood.

Police sirens sounded in the distance, and he hurried back to be with Trish and Raina. The ambulance and the fire truck came only minutes behind the two patrol cars. West Cole got out of one of the cars, along with his K-9.

"Where's Trish? Is she okay? The call came across the scanner. I hitched a ride with another officer."

"She's inside with Raina. She's pretty shook up. I've called an ambulance for her."

West was already halfway up the walkway. "I'll make sure the EMTs have a look at her." He disappeared inside the house.

Tanya would have brought a gun with her. Maybe Peanut could track her down. He took Peanut to the back of the house to look out on the houses that were under construction.

"Pea, find tools," Kenyon commanded.

Peanut lifted her nose in the air. At first, she seemed to be wandering, but then she kept circling back to one particular house that already had the siding up on it and would have provided a place to hide. It was possible one of the construction guys could have had a gun too.

He turned back to face the safe house. Where the half-built house was positioned, someone would have a clear view of the safe house kitchen window through the framed window that didn't have any glass in it yet.

When he stared at the concrete floor, his eye caught the glint of something shiny. A shell casing. Confirmation that Tanya had been here and taken a shot at the house? The glass in the windows was bulletproof so she would have been unsuccessful.

He picked up the shell casing to turn into forensics. "Come on, Sweet Pea, let's see if we can find her."

If the gun had been recently fired, that scent would remain in the air and on the person who had done the shooting for some time. The beagle led him outside and to a side street where trees blocked the view of the house before she lost the scent. Tanya must have had a car parked in the area.

She'd gotten away. Probably fled when she heard the sound of the sirens. He hurried back to the house. West sat with Trish while the EMT checked her out in the ambulance. Gus sat obediently outside the ambulance. The fire from the explosion had been extinguished, though the fire trucks lingered.

He walked over to the ambulance.

West leaned his head out. "She's going to be all right. We'll be going home for the rest of the day."

Kenyon called to one of the patrol officers who he didn't know very well. He must have been hired in the months after he he'd been in the explosion. "I could use an escort to the station. We'll be taking a woman and two young boys."

The officer nodded. "I'll tail you."

"Wait here. I'll bring them out." Kenyon stepped back into the house with Peanut, where Raina waited on the couch with Austin on her lap and Beacon leaning against her while she wrapped her arm around him. Chewy lay on the couch beside Beacon.

The picture of protection the sight created for him tugged at his heart. Raina still looked pale and in shock. He longed to gather her in his arms, to comfort her.

"Daddy." Austin spoke faintly without much enthusiasm.

Overwhelmed with love, he fell on his knees and spread his arms wide enough to embrace all three of them. "This whole thing has been awful and scary. I'm so sorry."

Beacon patted his cheek. "It's okay, Daddy."

Kenyon leaned back and touched Raina's cheek. "Thank you for being here with us."

The light seemed to have gone out of her eyes. "Is Trisha okay?"

"Relatively. West is taking her home for the rest of the

day." He rose to his feet. "We'll ride together in my car with a patrol car behind us. It's a short drive to the station."

The boys each picked up their backpacks. The other suitcases were in the driveway.

As they stepped out into the evening light and walked toward the car, Kenyon was grateful for the police presence. He found Raina's suitcase but not his. It could have been blown across the street or hung up in a bush.

He eyed the area all around the house. Tanya had been smart enough to figure out where the safe house was. She was escalating to the use of explosives.

He had to assume she might be watching the comings and goings at the police station. They couldn't stay there long and hope to be safe.

Once Raina and the twins were settled in the car, he drove the short distance to the police station, watching the cars around him and knowing that he couldn't drop his guard for even a second.

THIRTEEN

As they pulled into the parking lot of the police station, a heaviness descended on Raina. The explosion and the thought that Trish could have died had shaken her to the core. Her sister was the only family she had. The dream that she and Kenyon and the twins might be a family was clearly not going to happen.

What was all of this for if she was only going to be sidelined in the twins' lives and in Kenyon's? Perhaps she had been so committed to staying because she had held out hope that Kenyon would come to love her the way she loved him. She'd let go of that idea before when Kenyon had met his wife, she could do it again for the sake of the twins and for the sake of the friendship she and Kenyon shared. She didn't want to lose that too.

If this transition was going to happen, she needed to focus on how it could be done with the least amount of disruption to Beacon's and Austin's lives.

A petite woman with shoulder-length brown hair stood outside the station. A springer spaniel in a K-9 vest sat beside her. She waved as they pulled into the lot.

"Who is that?" Raina leaned a little closer to the windshield.

"That's Lucy Lopez. She's part of the task force but

works out of Fargo. The dog's name is Piper," said Kenyon. "I'm not sure why she's outside waiting for us."

Lucy and Piper approached the car as Raina and Kenyon got out and unloaded the boys from the back seat. Peanut and Chewy jumped out as well. Both the dogs ran to a grassy area to do their business.

"I'm in town to help out with the search for the gun shipment. Daniel told me about the explosion at the safe house. I just wanted you to know that Piper and I swept the parking lot and the building. Everything looks clean."

While he held Austin, Kenyon turned to face Raina, who held Beacon. "Piper's specialty is bomb detection."

The spaniel wagged her tail at the mention of her name.

"I'll walk you in." Lucy grabbed the bags from the back seat.

Raina liked the way the task force members looked out for each other.

Kenyon walked beside Lucy. "Any progress in finding out where the shipment is being kept?"

Lucy shook her head. "The task force has tails on both Hal and Brandon. Waiting on search warrants for some of the places they frequent."

"Something's got to turn up soon," said Kenyon.

"We're exercising extra caution since what happened to you and Daniel."

Raina wondered what Lucy was talking about.

They entered the building. Raina had been in here a few times before. Trish always enlisted her services as a baker when there was a celebration. She'd only been as far as the public administrative area though, where she always dropped off the treats. That part of the station was empty at this hour. No one sat behind the desks or the counter.

Lucy led them to a door that required an access code. She held the door open for them so they could step through.

"We'll probably just take over the break room on the second floor," said Kenyon.

"I'll be here for an hour or so until it's my turn to stake out Brandon's house. I imagine the graveyard shift for the PCPD will be coming and going."

It sounded to Raina like they'd have lots of help and protection. At the second floor, Lucy excused herself, saying that she would be on the third floor if they needed anything.

Kenyon led them to a room that had several couches, table and chairs and a microwave and fridge. The counter had a sink and a coffee maker.

The boys were already nodding off when they laid them down on the couch. Chewy settled down on the floor beside the twins. Once the boys were asleep and covered with a blanket, Kenyon pointed to the other couch and whispered, "You can sleep there if you like?"

"What about you?"

"There's a cot in the storage room I can bring out. I might just crash out on that chair later. I'm not tired right now. Think I'll take Peanut and go for a walk. I'll stay close. I won't leave this floor."

Raina slipped out of her coat, intending to use it as a blanket. When she laid down on the couch, she realized she was beyond exhausted, but she was too worked up to sleep. She sat up and wandered out into the hall, passing several closed doors.

She found Kenyon staring out a window that looked out on the parking lot. Peanut had put her front paws on the windowsill so she could watch too.

"Hey." He looked as weary as she felt. There was a soft quality to his voice.

She stood beside him and stared out at the parking lot. Traffic was light at this hour. The sky had grown dark. She always thought the city looked beautiful at night.

"I don't think Tanya will try anything tonight, even if she does know where we are." Kenyon crossed his arms over his chest.

"What did Lucy mean when she said that they were exercising extra caution in tailing those two brothers after what happened to you and Daniel?"

He turned to face her. "Brandon laid a trap for the task force while we were tailing him. We thought he was leading us to where the guns were being stored. Instead, there were men waiting for us. They shot an RPG at the car Daniel and I were in. We barely got out in time."

She reached to grab his sleeve. "Kenyon, you could've died. Why didn't you tell me?"

"I didn't want to worry you. You're dealing with enough already."

She saw in his actions enormous consideration for her feelings after having faced potential death.

He brushed his hand over her cheek. "I called you afterward. It was enough just to hear your voice." He turned sideways staring out the window. Peanut sat at his feet.

He drew strength just from hearing her voice? After her parents' death, it was Kenyon who helped her hold it together. That was when she realized she loved him. Maybe those feelings had been driven by how kind and supportive he'd been. Maybe it hadn't been love at all. They were good for each other as friends. She had to let go of the dream that they could be anything more.

"Kenyon, I've been thinking about what you said, about how when all this is over, I should move out." Her throat tightened as she spoke the words.

He turned to face her, his eyes searching hers. "That would be the best thing, don't you think?"

"I'm not sure what to say to that." The best thing would be if they were married and could be proper parents to Beacon and Austin, but she wanted a marriage based on love not practicality. "All I know is that we both love those boys and want the best for them. Maybe when you're working graveyard shifts or an intense investigation, they could stay with me. I can still do my job with them around. They liked helping me bake and going on deliveries."

He nodded. "Yes, I suppose that would work."

"You sound uncertain. I'm trying to come up with a viable solution here."

Kenyon placed his face in his hands. "I know the boys are safe with you and loved and cared for." He let out a heavy breath. "I know you're entitled to a life of your own."

It was clear he was worn-out. This wasn't a good time to have a serious conversation. "So I would be like a caring aunt who's ultra-involved in their lives. Is that how we would think of the arrangement?" She had to ask the question that had been dancing around the corner of her mind. "You don't think you'd ever remarry?" She would feel really displaced if he met someone else.

He shook his head. "Loving someone means risking losing them. I have had enough of that for a lifetime, and so have Beacon and Austin."

Now she understood the barrier Kenyon had set up around his heart. He didn't want to be married again, to her or anyone. The potential for the pain he'd been through once was just too great.

They both turned when they heard footsteps behind them.

Lucy came up the hall with Piper heeling beside her. "There you guys are. We've just got a report from the officers keeping an eye on Brandon. He's returned to the bowling alley on Wilson Street twice now. And Hal was spotted parked not too far from there earlier in the day."

"Yeah, Brandon stopped there when we were tailing him. Is that where they think the guns might be?"

She nodded. "The officers reported that Brandon just left, and the place is closed right now. Daniel put in for a search warrant when Brandon stopped there earlier. It's just now come through."

"This could be another trap."

"I know. Daniel says the search needs to happen tonight. He's on his way to the station right now, and so is West. He'll meet you in the conference room. I'm headed up there too." Her gaze rested on Raina. "I'll give you two a moment."

Lucy turned and went up the hallway, disappearing around a corner where there must be stairs or an elevator.

He turned back to face Raina. "You'll be all right here with the boys?"

She nodded. "Go and do your job. It doesn't get any more high-security than a police station. We'll be fine."

He leaned in and kissed her cheek. "I appreciate you so much."

She stood in the hallway watching Kenyon and Peanut disappear around the same corner that Lucy and Piper had.

She touched her fingers to her cheek. Kenyon had kissed her on the cheek many times before. It was just that now every touch, every look from him seemed to hold a different, more intense meaning than it had before for so many years.

It would be a struggle to quell the romantic thoughts she had about him, and she couldn't help her response to his touch, but she knew that would be the best thing for all of them. Kenyon was just too broken by all the losses he'd suffered to open his heart to love ever again.

* * *

Kenyon and Lucy had only been in the conference room for a few minutes when Daniel entered with his K-9 partner, Dakota. West and Gus were right behind him.

"Thanks, everyone, for coming. We have to search the bowling alley now. Both Brandon and Hal are back at their respective homes, and we have officers watching to make sure they don't leave again. Our informant heard that the guns will be moved out of the city tomorrow night. If the guns aren't in the bowling alley, we will miss our chance to catch these guys."

Kenyon shifted in his seat. "So we need to get the dogs in there to confirm that that's where the guns are being stored until transport?"

Daniel paced. "We interviewed the owner earlier today, and there is no reason to believe that he has any idea what his building is being used for."

"Just like the owners of the pizzeria," said Kenyon. Kenyon knew from the reports that after he'd been in the explosion, West had caught the first big break in the case when he discovered a shipment of guns being transported out of a Plains City pizza place. Though a former employee was connected to using the pizza place as storage for the guns, the owners had not had anything to do with the crime.

"There's a chance that even if the brothers themselves aren't watching the place, they have someone posted, so we need to strategize a way of getting in there without the risk of being seen." Daniel still hadn't sat down. He rested his hands on the back of one of the chairs.

"What do you suggest?" West asked.

"We travel to the site in one unmarked car with the dogs. Approach the back of the building. There are few places someone could hide in the alley and not be noticed. Lucy, you remain outside to warn of anything suspicious. West and Kenyon have the gun detecting dogs so they will do the search, and I will patrol to make sure no one pulls into that front lot."

"How big is this building?" Feeling as restless as Daniel acted, Kenyon rose to his feet as well.

Daniel flipped open a laptop that sat on the conference table. "We got the blueprints from the city."

Kenyon moved around to view the screen, as did Lucy and West.

"Two floors. Eight thousand square feet," said Lucy.

That was a lot of territory to cover in a short amount of time.

"It's unlikely the guns would be stashed in the area where the public would have access. We'll start with the offices and storage on the second floor." Daniel pointed to an area on the first floor. "There's a kitchen with a separate side entrance that has storage. That's a possibility."

Kenyon leaned closer to the screen. "Peanut and I can start with that area on the first floor."

"I'll take the second floor," said West.

"I can meet you up there if Peanut doesn't alert downstairs."

"Let's go. We got to move on this." Daniel had already lifted his coat from the back of the chair where he'd put it earlier. "Attach your radios. We've got officers three and four blocks away to move in if this thing goes south. The owner agreed to leave the back door unlocked. We'll lock up when we exit by that way."

"Let's roll," said Lucy.

As the four of them hurried downstairs and out into the parking lot, Kenyon glanced up to the second-floor window where he and Raina had stood only a short time ago. Of course, there was no one there now.

Daniel's words about the possibility of everything going south reminded him that he could die tonight. He thought that he should have given his sons one more hug. And Raina? Maybe he should have hugged her too. Why was he so conflicted about the decision he'd made to have her move out? They couldn't continue the living situation they were in. They'd talked about that even before Tanya Starling had disrupted their lives.

The team approached the unmarked police car.

Daniel opened the back hatch and commanded Dakota and Gus to jump in. Lucy sat in the passenger seat while Kenyon sat in the back with West, Peanut and Piper. Peanut fit on Kenyon's lap. He stroked the dog's soft head.

Several blocks away from the bowling alley, Daniel hit the blinker. He spoke into his radio. "One minute from the target."

Three officers answered back that they were in place.

The bowling alley was situated on a large corner lot with parking on three sides. Daniel parked on a side street. They would move in on foot. A car parked in an alley would be too much of a red flag.

Daniel turned to face Kenyon. "This is it. Get in and get out."

Kenyon nodded as his heartbeat ticked up a notch. This is what he loved about police work. He'd always thrived on the excitement. All three of them moved up the alley.

By the time Daniel, West and Kenyon entered the building with their K-9s, Lucy had deployed Piper. She slipped into the shadows by the building partially concealed by a dumpster that was low enough so she could still see anyone approaching from either side of the alley.

They entered the dark building and split off. The place smelled of sweat and stale beer. Even before he got to the kitchen, Peanut alerted by the counter where customers checked out shoes.

He found a gun in the drawer beneath the cash register.

He gave Peanut a treat. No time to play with the ducky that was her usual reward. The kitchen had a window with a shelf where people could pick up their food. He pushed through the door. Peanut paced in front of the grill and then sniffed the cupboards underneath the pop machine. Nothing.

Kenyon directed Peanut toward a door that he remembered from the blueprint looked like a storage area. Inside were shelves filled with boxes of food, jumbo-size jars of pickles and tomato sauce. Peanut sniffed all around with no alert. He opened the large walk-in freezer half-heartedly. An unlikely hiding place, but they had to search everywhere.

He pressed his radio. "Anything?"

"Not yet," said West.

"I'm headed up. There's nothing down here."

"I've covered two rooms on the east end."

"Come on, Sweet Pea." He moved out of the kitchen, back out into the open area where the lanes were.

Lucy's voice came across the radio. "Man just stepped into the alley."

Kenyon froze for only a second.

"Keep searching, Kenyon." Daniel's voice came through the radio. "Lucy, keep us apprised of the situation."

Peanut pulled on her leash, leading Kenyon toward the lanes.

"False alarm," said Lucy. "He wandered on through."

"Kenyon, where are you?"

"Peanut's on to something," responded Kenyon.

The beagle moved toward the end of the lane where the pins were set up, though there were none set up now. Peanut sat down and put her nose in the air. A clear alert. He leaned over and peered through but couldn't see much even when he activated the flashlight on his phone.

He spoke into his radio. "I think we got something."

There had to be a door that gave access to this part of the bowling alley. A quick search brought him to a dark corner and a small door. The space, which was a sort of hallway behind where the pins came down and were set up, had a low ceiling. Kenyon had to crouch to move through it. Peanut pulled hard on the lead. It took only a moment to find three wooden boxes secured with padlocks. The boxes had a spray-painted label on them that read Pins. It was unlikely that anyone would come back here, but if they did, they wouldn't think anything of the boxes.

Peanut swung her head and paced before sitting and lifting her nose in the air. The scent must be very strong. The guns must be in the wooden boxes.

"Good girl." He slipped her a treat.

Kenyon spoke into his radio. "We found them behind the bowling lanes."

Lucy's frantic voice disrupted the quiet. "The guy is coming back. You need to get out of there now."

Daniel's clipped voice came through the radio static. "No time."

Heart pounding, Kenyon moved farther down the hallway and slipped into the dark shadows of the far lane. Peanut nudged in beside him as he crouched.

He could hear footsteps getting louder. A door flung open and then a light was shone on the boxes. Kenyon pressed even harder against the back wall. If the man lifted the light a few inches, Kenyon's feet would be visible.

He held his breath. Peanut's soft fur brushed against his arm.

The man grunted and then said something under his breath that sounded like, "Safe and secure." Then he closed the door, causing the space to go black. Kenyon crouched for a long moment listening to the sound of his own breathing.

He could hear footsteps above him. He prayed that Daniel had found a suitable hiding space that accommodated a dog as big as Dakota. West and Gus were probably still on the second floor.

Minutes passed. He heard a heavy pounding and then the footsteps above him stopped.

His breath caught as he stared at the ceiling and prayed silently.

Please keep West and Gus safe.

Sweat dripped past his temple.

At least another five minutes went by before he heard the welcome sound of Lucy's voice. "He's gone."

"Let's clear out," said Daniel.

Kenyon shone his flashlight and worked his way back toward the undersized door. He stepped out into the silent dark alley and made his way back to the car.

Lucy was already waiting in the front passenger seat when he got there with Piper loaded in the back seat.

A few minutes later Daniel opened the back hatch for Dakota and Gus to jump in.

Daniel slipped behind the steering wheel while West got in the backseat. "Well done, you two."

Kenyon nodded. "Now all we have to do is set things up for tomorrow night when Brandon and Hal plan to move the guns." And pray they could catch the gun smuggling brothers once and for all.

FOURTEEN

As early morning light streamed through the closed window blinds, Raina pulled her coat she was using as a blanket tighter around her shoulders and opened her eyes. The boys were still asleep. The chair where Kenyon might have slept was empty.

Her throat went tight. Had something gone wrong with the mission last night?

She sat up and grabbed her phone to text him.

Is everything okay?

She stared at the phone as if the reply would be instantaneous. To her surprise, the text came within minutes.

Have coffee, will travel.

She shook her head. The connection between them, the bond they had from years of friendship was impossible to break. Why couldn't that be enough for them to be a couple?

"It just isn't, Raina," she whispered to herself.

She rose and stepped out into the hallway just in time for Kenyon to come around the corner. Peanut must be in the kennel in back of the building.

He handed her a paper cup with a lid. "We have an espresso maker upstairs. I know you like your lattes."

"Thanks. Did you get any sleep?"

"Yes." He pointed at the cot with a thin blanket on it just around the corner. "I thought it best if I slept where I would know right away if anyone came onto this floor. For safety, and I didn't want to wake you or the boys when I got back."

He'd positioned the cot, so he had a view of the elevator and the stairwell.

She took a sip of the warm sweet liquid. "How did it go last night?"

"Actually, pretty good. We're going to set up a sting to try and catch the kingpins in the act of transporting weapons. Intel tells us it should happen tonight." He leaned against the wall. "I'd like to get you and the boys moved to someplace safe today."

"I know we can't stay here long-term. What are we going to do? Order takeout every day?" Even that would look suspicious to someone watching the comings and goings in the building when there were restaurants within walking distance.

As secure as the police station was, it wasn't practical to stay here. Keeping the boys clean and fed and confined to the break room would be close to impossible. "Where would we go? Isn't the other safe house still in use?"

"Yes, but I spoke to my uncle. He's open to you staying at his ranch. It has a level of security because of how far out of town it is. Of course, we'll have an officer posted. The boys have been there before and loved it, so it will be one less new thing they have to deal with."

The ranch held fond memories for Raina. "How are we going to guarantee that we're not followed?"

"Trish will escort the boys out first along with another

officer. They will go out the back by the K-9 training facility. Then you will leave with me dressed in a police uniform." Kenyon took a sip of his coffee. "The PCPD already did a sweep of the area around the building. No sign of Tanya."

"She could be hiding in any one of the buildings around here." The PCPD building was situated in the center of town with lots of other businesses surrounding it.

Kenyon nodded. "There's no way we could search every possibility or even gain access without a warrant."

She knew that any plan held a level of risk, but she was confident if she was with Kenyon she'd be in good hands. "I understand what needs to happen. Just tell us when and where to be."

"We need to get this done this morning. Many members of the task force are being called in to deal with this sting, and we have to start the planning as soon as possible."

"First things first, let's go explain to Beacon and Austin what is going to happen in a way a three-year-old can understand."

"You're good at that." He cupped her elbow as they turned the corner and headed back up the hallway.

His touch still made her wither. "You do a good job too. I think it works best if we talk to them together."

Beacon leaned out of the door and grinned when he saw them. Chewy poked his head out as well.

"Hey, sleepyhead." Warmth filled her heart at the sight of his smile. The boy and the puppy toddled toward her. "We have quite a big day," she said as she lifted him up into her arms.

After putting a makeshift breakfast together from the vending machine for the boys and telling them they were going to go to Uncle Charlie's farm, they took the elevator down the stairs to the first floor, where Trish waited with another Plains City officer.

Austin turned to face Kenyon and Raina. "Why can't you come with us?"

The look of confusion on his face nearly broke Raina's heart. She kneeled and gathered him into her arms, holding him close. "I'll be there with you in just a little bit."

Beacon pressed close to his brother, reaching out to gather a strand of Raina's red hair. "We'll miss you, Raina."

Kenyon kneeled as well. "Boys, Raina will be there soon, and Uncle Charlie said he'd saddle up a horse for you."

Their eyes brightened at the idea.

Trish stepped closer to them. "Come on, guys."

Raina and Kenyon watched from a window as Trish and the other police officer escorted the boys to an unmarked police car. The male officer remained close to the boys as they walked holding Trish's hands. Chewy lumbered behind with his nose in the air. They would be out in the open for only a few minutes before being secured in the car.

After they were all loaded up, Trish gave a wave from the driver's seat before backing out.

Raina released the tightness in her stomach with a deep breath. "I don't like being away from them, especially under these circumstances."

From the window where they watched, Kenyon leaned close to her, his shoulder touching hers.

"They don't like being away from you either." His voice had taken on a flat quality, like he was thinking about something.

"We should pray, Kenyon."

He nodded. She turned to face him, and he took her hands in his.

"Lord, we pray Beacon and Austin arrive at the farm safe. And for Raina as well."

Raina added, "Be with the team today and tonight as they put together and execute the plan to take these gun traffickers out."

The prayer calmed her frayed nerves.

He squeezed her hands. Something he'd done a hundred times before when they prayed together, but something felt different. When she opened her eyes, the warmth she saw in his gaze made her heart flutter. He still hadn't let go of her hands.

What was going on with him? How did he really feel?

He stepped back breaking the moment between them. "Officer Lopez brought in one of her uniforms. I think you're about the same size."

He turned and headed up the hallway toward the elevator.

Feeling confused about the way Kenyon was acting, Raina followed. Her stomach had twisted into a tight knot. She prayed the plan would work and she could get safely to the twins.

Kenyon waited outside the women's locker room while Raina got into the borrowed uniform. Peanut sat at his feet. When the twins had said goodbye, he'd seen how much they depended on Raina to help them process their feelings just like a mom would.

In that moment when she was holding his sons, he thought she was more beautiful than ever before. Would it even work for her to become a devoted aunt to them? The turmoil over the decision made his stomach tight. He wanted what was best for everybody involved.

Raina stepped out of the locker room. Her hair had been

pulled up in a tight bun with a police hat placed on it, pulled down low to partially cover her face. Her red hair was no longer visible.

She spread her hands wide, green eyes holding light like the morning sun. "How do I look?"

Like a million bucks.

He stepped closer to her. "Like a genuine Plains City police officer." He grabbed the utility belt he'd borrowed. It was lighter than a police issue one but had enough on it to fool someone seeing Raina from a distance. The holster had an unloaded gun. "Here, put this on."

He handed it to her. When she fumbled with the buckle, he moved in to help her. His face was very close to hers. He could smell her floral perfume.

He clicked the buckle in place. "There."

He lifted his head. His gaze met hers.

"Kenyon." She uttered his name in a breathy tone, her eyes searching his.

He leaned close and covered her mouth with his, gathering her into his arms. The kiss was not rushed, not impulsive.

He pulled away but rested his fingers on her cheek, relishing the intensity and warmth he saw in her eyes. "I've been thinking."

"Yes." Her expression filled with expectation.

He took a step back. Fear stabbed at his awareness as a million what-ifs whirled through his head. What if they couldn't make it work as a couple? That would devastate Beacon and Austin even more than they had been. What if something happened to Raina too? Life could turn on a dime and things could be taken away as easily as they'd been given. He looked away. "Maybe we shouldn't rush your moving out."

Her features took on a little harder edge, communicating confusion. "Okay?"

The change in her expression told him that she had expected him to say something different. He had wanted to say that he loved her, but fear held him prisoner.

Officer Jenna Morrow poked her head in the room. "You better get going. Daniel wants to start the planning meeting by ten."

"Almost ready," said Kenyon. "We'll be out of here in the next few minutes."

Jenna nodded and disappeared.

"You've got a lot on your mind," said Raina.

This woman had the patience of Job. "Why don't we talk some on the drive?" He didn't regret kissing her this time.

Lucy and Piper met them at the door. "Your patrol vehicle is all ready to go. Piper didn't pick up on any bomb materials."

"Thanks, Lucy." Tension knotted through his chest as he stepped out into the open. He whispered to Raina, "Don't be looking around for her. Remember you're a cop."

Raina took in an audible breath and nodded. She squared her shoulders but kept her head turned toward the side to avoid being recognized from a distance.

Peanut fell in beside him. There were other officers arriving and leaving in the side lot where many of the vehicles were parked. He was grateful for the distraction of other people. The patrol car they'd be taking was his regular K-9 vehicle, but his car number had been altered in case Tanya was tracking that.

He loaded up Peanut while Raina got in the passenger seat.

When he got behind the wheel, he hesitated for a moment, remembering that the bomb on Trisha's car had been triggered by the starter.

Raina leaned closer and touched his arm. "Lucy said it was all clear."

Only her touch helped relax his clenched stomach. "I know." Taking in a sharp breath, he turned the key in the ignition. The warm hum of the engine filled the air around him.

Peanut let out a strange half bark just as he shifted into Reverse.

The sound was one of distress.

He turned his head to look at her. "What's going on, Sweet Pea?"

A second later, three loud booms filled the air, one right after the other. His vehicle lifted on its side and swung in a half circle.

Raina let out a scream.

When he looked through his windshield, a fireball took up much of the parking lot. Flames shot out of one of the patrol cars. Black smoke filled the air. Police officers scattered, some running toward the building and others seeking to help one officer who lay on the pavement.

At least three bombs had exploded one right after the other. Tanya's work, no doubt. Tanya couldn't pinpoint where Raina was, so she targeted the whole parking lot. For what purpose? As a distraction. Maybe to breach the building.

The smoke grew thicker and blacker. Lucy was doing regular sweeps with Piper. The bomb must have been placed right after a sweep.

That meant Tanya was close. "Get out. There might be more bombs."

FIFTEEN

By the time she jumped out of the passenger seat, Raina was coughing. Her eyes burned from the smoke. She couldn't see much, but she heard yelling, footsteps and the crackling of flames.

Her heart pounded as she moved around the front of the vehicle, placing a hand on the hood to guide her. The metal was hot from the intensity of the blast. Heat pressed on her right side where the explosion had taken place and several fires still burned.

She heard Kenyon command Peanut to jump out.

The chaos and the smoke disoriented her.

"Kenyon."

His hand found hers. "This way. We need to get you inside."

Someone brushed by her, hitting her shoulder. The wail of the fire trucks in the distance filled the air.

Inhaling the smoke made her lightheaded. She coughed so badly it caused her to bend over. Clutching her chest, she let go of Kenyon's hand. Several people bumped into her as they ran by. She lifted her head.

The smoke had grown so thick she could no longer see Kenyon. When she called his name, it was drowned out by the approaching sirens of the fire truck. The ambulances had already arrived. When the smoke cleared momentarily, she saw a flash of a paramedic's uniform. Muffled shouts bombarded her from all sides.

She turned one way and then the other. When she lifted her head, she could see the upper floors of the PCPD, though the first floor was obscured by smoke.

She rushed toward the building, seeking refuge from the smoke. Her police hat fell off in the process and her red hair became visible.

She thought she heard Peanut's distinct bark. Turning slightly, she called Kenyon's name again but ended up coughing.

A hand was placed on her back. "Here, let me help you." She caught a glimpse of an EMT vest.

The voice was female. The hand guided her away from where she wanted to go.

She coughed. "I need to get inside." She pointed but ended up bent over coughing.

"This way." The EMT tightened her hold on Raina's arm.

Raina turned to look at the EMT. Shock and fear spread like wildfire through her. Tanya Starling.

The face that looked at her was filled with rage. "Hello, Raina."

Fighting off the rising panic, Raina moved to get away. Tanya's grip on her arm was iron tight. Tanya slapped a piece of cloth on Raina's face, covering her nose. Raina took in a breath as she tried to move her head away.

Chloroform.

She felt herself collapsing, falling down an abyss. The world spun around her, but she never hit hard ground. Instead she had the sensation of floating right before she lost consciousness…

When she came to, her cheek was pressed against dirty carpet, and she felt the sensation of rocking back and forth. She glimpsed windows that were covered with paper. She was being transported in some kind of a van. When she went to move her hands, she saw that they were bound in front of her.

Tanya was taking her somewhere. Why hadn't she been killed on the spot? Too many witnesses maybe? What did she have planned?

Raina tilted her head, trying to see what was around her. The back of the van was empty. She lifted her head a little higher for a view of the back of Tanya's head.

When she tried to free her hands, it was clear that would be a futile activity without some kind of cutting tool. The rope was thick and tied with no give in it at all.

The drive seemed to last forever. At one point, it felt like they were going uphill on a winding road.

Finally, the van came to a stop. Tanya got out, slamming the door.

Raina waited in the silence, wondering what was going to happen next. Her heartbeat thrummed in her ears.

She managed to push herself up to her knees. By lifting her head and stretching her neck, she could see out the front window. Tanya had driven to a yurt surrounded by rocks and trees.

Walking on her knees, she moved toward the sliding side door to see if she could open it.

The door handle on the van was rattled. Raina made a split-second decision to fake still being unconscious, thinking that might allow her to surprise Tanya and escape or subdue her in some way. She flopped back down on the dirty carpet, rolled on her side and closed her eyes.

The side door slid open.

Tanya shook Raina's shoulder.

"Come on. Don't tell me you're still out cold."

Tanya slammed the side door and moved around to the back doors, opening them. Raina opened her eyes a slit to get a read on where Tanya was.

Tanya reached for Raina's feet. When Tanya's head was close to them, Raina lifted her foot and smacked Tanya on the underside of her chin.

The momentum of the blow caused Tanya to whirl to the side, but she swung around quickly to grab Raina by the shoulders as she tried to get out of the van.

Blood stained Tanya's mouth. She must have bitten her tongue when Raina kicked her.

Still halfway in the van, Raina tried to roll away, but she was no match for Tanya's strength.

Tanya grabbed Raina's collar and pulled her close to her face. "You will cooperate. Do you understand me?"

The rage Raina saw in Tanya's eyes was terrifying.

"Yes," Raina responded in a trembling voice.

"Now stand up and walk."

Raina put her feet on the ground and stood up. Tanya closed the van doors and pushed on Raina's back.

Raina walked with her hands bound in front of her. There was no sign of another cabin or a camper anywhere. Tanya had brought her out to the middle of nowhere.

Once Kenyon realized what had happened...if Kenyon realized what had happened, how would he ever find her?

She had to find a way to escape this unstable woman before she was killed.

Kenyon stumbled into the PCPD building with Peanut by his side.

Captain Ross rose from where he'd been sitting next to an officer who looked like he'd been outside when the explosion happened. The officer had dirt smudges on his face and his uniform was torn at the shoulder.

"Kenyon, what is it?"

"I think Raina has been abducted by Tanya Starling."

He could barely get the words out. "She was disguised as an EMT."

When he'd gotten separated from Raina, he'd searched for her. He caught only a glimpse of her red hair before the van door closed. He ran toward the van as Tanya got behind the wheel. The van had gotten up to speed and exited the parking lot before he could catch it.

"Which way did she go?"

"Up the street toward the four-way stop." Kenyon shook his head, feeling a sense of desperation. How could he let this happen? By the time he got back to his vehicle, Tanya was long gone. "Has there been any reporting of a shooting in town or anything that might indicate Tanya was involved in harming Raina?"

The captain shook his head. "Things have been chaotic because of the explosion, but I don't think any major calls have come in."

That didn't mean Raina was still alive. It just meant no one had reported seeing anything suspicious. Kenyon paced and combed his fingers through his dark hair. "Maybe Tanya has some sort of remote location in mind where there are no witnesses. Raina could be anywhere." An idea hit him. "We need to get in touch with her accomplice. He might know where she would take Raina. I heard he was out on bail. The judge said there wasn't enough evidence to charge him with attempted kidnapping. He was concerned that Vernon was misled by Tanya."

"His contact information will be on the arrest form. Let's go upstairs to my office," said Ross.

The two men hurried upstairs where Captain Ross pulled up the file. When Ross called Vernon Cunningham's cell, there was no answer.

"Try the dojo," said Kenyon.

Ross pressed in the number. While it rang, he studied Kenyon, pointing at his face. "Are you okay?"

Kenyon touched his forehead. His fingers were bloody. He must have knocked his head on something at some point. "I'll live. We have to find Raina."

A voice came across the line. Ross turned his attention to the phone. "Yes, hello, I'm looking for Vernon Cunningham... He is, good. Can you get him to come to the phone? It's a police matter."

Kenyon took in a breath. "He's there."

Please God, help us find Raina.

"Mr. Cunningham, this is Captain Douglas Ross of the Plains City Police. It seems that your friend Tanya Starling may have abducted a woman. Do know anything about this?" Doug adjusted his silver-framed glasses while he listened to the response. "So you don't know anything about this potential kidnapping?... Let me remind you that we have reasonable cause to come down and search that dojo... Okay, then can you tell us where else she might have gone?"

Captain Ross listened and nodded and then grabbed a piece of paper and a pen to write something down. "Thank you. Your cooperation with the police has been noted in light of the charges against you." He pressed the disconnect button.

"What did he say?"

"He said that the dojo owns a yurt that is used for training retreats. It's a ways out of town up in the Black Hills."

That fit with the direction he'd seen Tanya going, but it was at least a twenty-minute drive to get there. "That was his only idea where she might have gone?"

Ross nodded.

What if they were wrong? What if she wasn't there?

"I need to get up there. Can you spare anyone to back me up?"

Doug ran his hand over his balding head. "We're several officers down because of the explosion. Let me see if I can get someone lined up." He handed Kenyon the piece of paper he'd written on. "This is where she's at."

Kenyon stared at the paper. He knew the road that led to this location, though it must be quite high up the mountain as he didn't remember ever seeing a yurt.

Daniel probably couldn't release anyone from the task force either, as they'd be late in getting back for the planning session.

"I can't wait. Raina's life depends on finding her quickly." He didn't want to live in a world without his best friend... and the woman he loved.

"Kenyon, you need backup."

Kenyon was already moving toward the door with Peanut trotting beside him. "Let me know when you get some."

He hurried downstairs and out to his car. The fires had been extinguished and much of the smoke had cleared. Fire trucks remained in the lot, but the ambulances had all left. Though his SUV had been lifted off its wheels by the blast, it appeared to be functional.

He picked Peanut up and put her in the passenger seat. No time to load her in the kennel. Kenyon drove out of the PCPD parking lot. Peanut sat against the back of the seat and lifted her head to see out the side window. It calmed his frayed nerves to have his partner in the seat next to him.

He stroked her soft head. "Best partner ever. You've been through a few things yourself." Peanut had been at the explosion that had robbed him of his memory.

He drove through town and out toward the Black Hills, praying that Raina had been taken to the yurt, and that Tanya hadn't killed her yet.

SIXTEEN

Tanya pushed Raina into the yurt and led her toward a folding camp chair. At least ten cots were set up inside the round space. The center of the yurt had a woodstove with some cooking supplies stacked beside it on a small table.

Raina glanced around, looking for some weapon or way of escape. She had to get her hands untied or getting away would be almost impossible. She took note of the steak knife on the table beside the cast iron pan.

Tanya shoved Raina into a folding camp chair. A bulge beneath the EMT vest indicated that Tanya had a gun.

Tanya paced the floor and then turned and pointed at Raina. "You're not Joey's mother. Say it."

Now Raina understood why she'd been dragged up here, why there had been a delay in killing her. Tanya needed Raina to confirm her distorted view of reality.

"I'm not Joey's mother." That was easy enough to say.

"Good, so give Joey back to me so we can be a family again."

"The boy you tried to kidnap is not Joey. His name is Beacon."

"You took Joey from me." Tanya pulled her gun out and placed it under Raina's chin.

Raina winced as the barrel of the gun pressed against her skin.

Tanya leaned close. Her eyes had a wild quality. "You're not his mother. Say it."

"I said it already." Tears filled Raina's eyes. She wasn't Beacon's mother either. As much as she wanted to be, she wasn't. "You have to let go of this ridiculous fantasy."

Tanya pulled the gun away from Raina's face and stood up. "Joey deserves to be with his family." Agitation colored her words.

Would speaking reality to Tanya push her over the edge or help her to see how messed up her choices were? "Tanya, your mother and father are dead and so is Joey. He died ten years ago at Wind Cave."

Tanya's eyes glazed as she shook her head. With the gun still in her hand, she paced.

Raina's whole body tensed as she braced for what Tanya might do next.

Raina's assertions seemed to be upsetting her more.

Tanya stopped and lifted her head. She turned toward the door. "What's that sound?"

Raina didn't hear anything. "I don't know."

Tanya hurried outside.

This was her chance. Raina rose quickly and grabbed the knife. She sawed it over the rope, grateful that the knife was sharp enough that it cut almost all the way through quickly.

Tanya was coming back toward the open door of the yurt. Raina dropped the knife off to the side where a stack of firewood partially hid it.

Tanya swooped down on Raina, panic written all over her face. "Get up. We're going."

"What? Why?"

Whatever Tanya had seen or heard outside had scared

her. Raina tried to pull and twist the rope to break the final strands without Tanya noticing. Tanya led her out a back door where a steep trail was. Raina hesitated.

Tanya pulled the gun and pushed it into Raina's back. "Walk."

With Tanya behind her, Raina continued to twist the rope to free herself. The final strand broke, but she kept her arms close to her body and held on to the rope so Tanya wouldn't see. The trail was steep enough that Tanya had to holster her gun.

Raina pretended to stumble so she could bend to grab a branch close to the trail. She swung around, hitting Tanya across the face with it. The move momentarily stunned Tanya, allowing Raina to get away.

She climbed up the trail that had become rockier and even steeper. She bent over and pulled herself up by grabbing protruding rocks. Tanya was maybe ten feet behind her. When she reached for a handhold on a large rock, it came loose and rolled hitting other rocks, causing a mini avalanche that forced Tanya to stop and step aside.

Raina kept climbing until she came to the top of the trail that had a steep drop-off on the other side. The trail was narrow. She ran along the ridge. Tanya was still some distance behind her but closing in. The woman was very athletic.

Tanya lifted the gun and fired. Because she was moving and shooting at the same time, the shot went wild. Raina dove off into the rocky forest that led back down to the yurt. Though not as steep as the cliff-like side of the trail, it was still hazardous because of the rocks and angle of the hill.

She moved toward bushes that would provide a degree of cover. Raina stumbled and fell. When she glanced up the hill, Tanya was taking aim. There was no time to move out of the line of fire. She flattened herself against the rocks.

Tanya aimed her gun, holding it with both hands as she lifted it, taking a small step backward. Her arms flew up like she was a bird about to take flight. Then she disappeared.

Raina's breath caught. Tanya had fallen off the cliff.

Raina scrambled up the mountain. By the time she reached the top, she was out of breath. She peered over the edge.

Tanya was holding on to a ledge with one shoe precariously resting on a small foothold. The gun had fallen on the rocks below her.

Raina dropped on her belly and reached down. Her arms were not long enough. She grabbed a nearby sturdy looking branch.

"Grab hold of this, and I'll pull you up," said Raina.

Tanya glanced down at the rocks below her and then looked up at Raina. "Let me die. Just let me die."

"I can't do that," said Raina.

"It was me. It was my fault Joey died. I should have been watching him closer."

"Tanya, it was just an accident. Please take the branch."

"My parents hated me after that. They blamed me."

"No, Tanya, please take the branch."

"Mom said as much to me in the hospital before she died. I ruined the family."

"Your life matters," Raina pleaded.

"You're helping me after I tried to kill you?" She shook her head in disbelief.

Tanya's foot slipped. Rocks tumbled below her as her foothold gave way, and she grabbed hold of another rock.

Her feet swung wildly before finding a small protrusion to rest her toes on. Her hold was precarious.

"Please. I can see you want to live, or you would have let go." Raina leaned over even farther to get the branch closer to Tanya.

Tanya gazed up at Raina for a long moment before grabbing hold of the branch with one hand and then the other. Raina stood up to get more leverage. She pulled while Tanya found footholds. When she got close to the top, Raina reached a hand out to her and pulled her the final distance.

Tanya fell against her chest. She was weeping so intensely that her body shook. "It was all my fault."

Raina wrapped her arms around the woman. "No, you were just a kid." The anguish she heard in Tanya's voice made her throat go tight.

Tanya's voice sounded like that of a little girl. "I'll make it right, Mommy. I promise. I'll make it right."

Raina made shushing sounds and stroked Tanya's hair. "It's going to be okay." She held Tanya until the crying became less intense realizing that she was not holding a grown woman but a twelve-year-old child who had been consumed by guilt.

When she looked up, Kenyon was at the far end of the trail where they had come up with his gun drawn.

Kenyon let his shooting arm go limp by his side, though he did not holster his weapon. The scene of tenderness between the two women was not the one he'd expected. Raina was holding and comforting Tanya. What was going on?

Raina held her hand up, signaling that he needed to stay where he was. Peanut, who had made the climb up the steep hill with him, sat at his feet.

She helped Tanya get to her feet before stepping free

of the hug, then she held Tanya's face in her hands, saying something to her. Tanya nodded and then turned and walked back up the trail toward Kenyon.

Kenyon stared down the cliff at the yurt where his backup had just pulled into place behind his squad car.

Within five minutes of Kenyon leaving the city, Ross had radioed that he'd found Kenyon some backup.

Tanya approached Kenyon.

"She's ready to be taken into custody." Raina put her hand on Tanya's shoulder.

Tanya nodded as her eyes glazed. "I just wanted the happy family we were before Joey died back."

He wasn't sure if he could trust what was happening. Tanya had shown herself to be quite erratic. As a detective, he didn't have handcuffs.

"Tanya, you go first. I'll be right behind you. Raina will go last." If Tanya was going to try anything, he wanted to be a barrier between her and Raina.

He pulled his gun and kept it trained on Tanya's back.

Tanya made her way down the rocky hill. Peanut lagged behind choosing her path carefully.

When they got to the bottom and circled around to the front of the yurt, the other officer was waiting outside his vehicle.

"Cuff this woman and take her into the station to be processed," said Kenyon.

The officer moved to pull his cuffs off his belt. Tanya whirled around, approaching Raina.

Kenyon reached for his gun.

Tanya wrapped her arms around Raina's neck. "Thank you for saving my life."

"You're welcome."

The officer cuffed Tanya and led her to the patrol car.

Kenyon and Raina watched as the officer got turned around on the narrow mountain road and disappeared around a curve.

Kenyon turned to face Raina. "What happened?"

"She was a tormented soul, a woman consumed by guilt. Maybe she was unstable to begin with, and the accident with her brother pushed her over the edge."

"What did she mean that you saved her life?"

"She slipped off the cliff. I pulled her up."

"Amazing."

"I suppose. It was only something God could orchestrate."

He touched her arm. "No, I meant, you're amazing. You saved the life of someone who tried to kill you."

She lifted her head toward him. "It's over, isn't it? We can go back to…to what, Kenyon? We never did get the chance to finish our conversation."

"I had time to think on the drive up here. I just couldn't picture my world without you."

"What are you saying?"

"I've let fear control me. Afraid that I would lose your friendship. Afraid to admit I loved you because that meant there was a possibility that I could lose you because we couldn't make it work romantically." He sucked in a breath that was almost painful and looked at her. "And then I thought, what if you die just like Monique did. I don't know if I could go through that again."

"Oh, Kenyon." She touched his cheek and then pressed her forehead against his. "There's always risk in choosing to love someone, not just of loss but there's the risk of pain."

"I know I've caused you some of that. I'm so sorry."

She tilted her head to look up at him. "It's worth the risk though, don't you think? To love and to be loved in a deep and connected way. I think we understand God so much better when we choose to love."

"I'm ready to take a chance, Raina. You should move back to your house and we can date. Let's see if we can make this work. For us and for the twins."

"Oh, Kenyon. I would love that." A soft smile spread across her face.

He rubbed his thumb on her cheek, relishing the light that had come into her green eyes. Then he bent his head and kissed her. She rested one hand on his chest and wrapped the other around the back of his neck.

His lips lingered on her mouth as he put an arm around her waist and pulled her close. After a long moment, he lifted his head but continued to look into her eyes. He could stay here forever.

"We could be good together, Kenyon. A true family."

"I know no one will ever love those boys more than you do."

"Yes, that's true, but I love you too. I have for a long time."

"Sorry I was so slow to see that." He kissed her again.

His radio crackled and he took a step back.

Daniel's voice came through the speaker. "Hey, I just heard the news. Tanya was taken into custody without a single shot fired."

"Yes, it's quite a story how that happened." He gazed at Raina.

"I hate to remind you, but we've got a sting to set up and you and Peanut are key players."

A look of fear played across Raina's face. She turned slightly away from him.

"Give me half an hour. I'm on my way back to the station house." He clicked the disconnect button and gathered

Raina in his arms to kiss her one more time. Hoping to calm her fears, he wrapped his arms around her and held her.

She pulled away first. "I know you have to get back to work." Her voice had a flat quality to it.

"Let's get off this mountain," he said. "Do you want to spend the day at the farm with the boys? I can arrange for a ride once we get to the station." He wished it could be him taking her out there, but there was no time.

"That's a good idea. The boys love it out there." She stared down the mountain. "It will be nice not to have to be looking over my shoulder."

He still had a long day that would go into the night ahead of him. He didn't need to ask her why she had become subdued and distant. They were both thinking the same thing.

He could die tonight.

SEVENTEEN

As Uncle Charlie's farm came into view, Raina had mixed emotions. She was excited to see Beacon and Austin, to hug them and know that they were all safe. She only wished that Kenyon was with her, that his mission was over.

The revelation that he wanted to give a romantic relationship a chance was a balm to her soul. She saw now that she would have to take her own words to heart. Loving someone meant risking the pain of losing them.

Kenyon and the team were going into a dangerous situation.

The officer who was driving her pulled up to the main farmhouse. She had made the decision to stay at the farm until she heard how the sting had gone. This was a place of good memories for the twins, a place where they felt safe. In the back of her mind, she knew if they were going to get bad news about Kenyon or any member of the team, being out here in the country surrounded by all this beauty would somehow cushion the blow.

She could see the boys peering out the window. By the time she got out of the patrol car, they'd run outside onto the porch with Uncle Charlie behind them. Trish as well came out on the porch holding Gabriel. West would be on the mission tonight too. She and Trish needed to be together during this time.

She gathered the boys into her arms. "My two favorite guys."

"And Daddy?" said Beacon.

"And Daddy," said Raina. "He's my favorite too." She stared into his blue eyes, so much like his father's.

Maybe someday, the boys would call her mom.

"We got to feed the goats." Austin swiveled his tennis-shoe-clad foot and pointed toward a barn in the distance.

"You did?" Raina glanced up at Uncle Charlie, who gave her a wink. He was a leathered looking man with curly salt and pepper hair.

"We're just getting lunch ready," said Trish. "Come on, guys, let's go inside and finish up."

Beacon grabbed Raina's hand, swinging it back and forth as they headed up the stairs. Austin ran ahead, following after Uncle Charlie and peppering him with questions about the farm animals.

When they were on the porch and the others had gone inside, Beacon let go of her hand. "Raina, I wish Daddy was here. He likes the farm."

She kneeled to get down on his level. "Me too, little one."

"Raina, I like you so much." He patted both her cheeks with his hands.

"I like you too, kiddo." Maybe someday they would truly be a family. So much hung in the balance right now. The boys had only been a year old when their mother died. Though Kenyon had worked to keep her memory alive by showing them photos, they didn't really understand what it meant to have a mom.

Raina walked into the kitchen with Beacon. The others had already settled down to eat their sandwiches and potato chips.

Uncle Charlie sat with them, making jokes about how some of the potato chips were shaped like animals.

From where she stood at the counter with the sandwich ingredients in front of her, Trish studied her sister for a long moment. "Do you want something to eat?"

"In just a minute. I need to freshen up first." Raina excused herself and entered the downstairs bathroom. After washing her hands, she splashed water on her face, hoping the cold water would stave off some of the anxiety that threaded through her. As she dried her face, she glimpsed herself in the mirror. Her eyes looked tired.

When she stepped out of the bathroom, Trish was there. She wrapped her arms around Raina.

"I know this is hard thinking about what the task force might face tonight."

"It can't be any easier for you being married to a police detective."

"I've had a little practice," said Trish.

Raina stood back as tears flowed down her cheeks. "Kenyon said that he was open to us dating, trying to make it work as a couple."

Trish tugged on her sister's sleeve. "That's great news."

"I guess, but really bad timing. What if I lose him just as he was willing to open his heart to me?"

Trish hugged her again. "That task force is the best of the best."

"That doesn't mean bad things can't happen."

"I know, but this is what it means to be married to a cop. You're getting a taste of it before you have to fully commit."

If things worked out between her and Kenyon. This would be her life. Long nights spent worrying if he would come home. "I'm just glad you're here with me."

Trish gave Raina a sideways hug. "Let's go give those boys a nice day at the farm."

She'd have to work to hide her anxiety, but that was part of what she needed to do to give the twins a safe world if she was going to become their mom.

That was a big *if*.

As the night grew darker, Kenyon waited in his unmarked car, with Peanut in the passenger seat, for the radio signal to move into place in the bowling alley. The business had closed at ten. A spotter and sniper from the PCPD were in position on a building across the street. Another officer watched the back of the bowling alley from an apartment building. Officers and members of the task force waited two and three blocks away in unmarked cars to move in if needed.

Though the bowling alley was closed, a car had pulled into the lot at one point and drove in a circle before leaving. The officer watching from the empty apartment had identified a man sitting in his car with a view to the alley and the back entrance. It appeared that the brothers had sent men to watch the place.

The plan was that Kenyon, West and Jenna would enter the building before Brandon and Hal showed up. Kenyon would get into position at the end of the narrow passageway behind the bowling lanes to radio the others once Brandon and Hal had pulled the boxes of guns. His job was to be sure that it was Brandon and Hal doing the dirty work. Catching more low-level guys was not the goal here.

Jenna's K-9, who was trained in suspect apprehension, would take them down hopefully inside the building. If not, Daniel and Lucy would be waiting in the alley. Zach was in a car on the street watching the front and ready to jump out if needed.

The night had worn on without anything happening and no chance to move into the building without being spotted by the sentry. The posted man watching the alley was the only indication that the brothers might show up. If they suspected a sting at all, then Hal and Brandon would back off and all the preparation to catch them red handed would be for nothing. Kenyon prayed that this wasn't another setup to take out task force members.

"Looks like our guy in the car has gotten out and is walking over to the convenience store." The voice was that of the officer in the apartment building.

Kenyon shifted in his seat and reached for the door handle. The convenience store was on a side street two blocks away. He must be going to get something to eat or use the bathroom. They had maybe ten minutes to get in place without being spotted.

"All clear on the front," said the spotter on the roof.

"Go, go, go," said Daniel through the radio.

Kenyon opened the door. Peanut jumped out after him. He hurried up the alley and through the back door. Jenna and West followed. Kenyon hurried through a room where boxes and a broken jukebox and a popcorn machine were stored, making his way toward the back part of the bowling alley. He opened the small door that allowed him to access where the guns were hidden.

Kenyon clicked his flashlight on and off quickly to orient himself before seeking a hiding place at the end of the hallway. His heart sank.

He turned his head sideways and pushed the talk button on his radio. "The guns are not here."

He could almost feel the drop in mood even though nobody said anything on the radio in response to the news.

Peanut whined and lifted her head.

"Wait a sec. Let's not call it off just yet. Peanut's trying to tell me something and that sentry is out there for a reason." He lifted his finger from the talk button. "Tools. Find tools."

Peanut put her nose to the ground. Kenyon followed as Peanut lead him back into the kitchen and into the storage room he'd previously searched. The dog lifted her nose. Then she put her paws on one of the shelves before sitting and lifting her head.

"Up here?" Kenyon moved toward the shelf, seeing only boxes with food labels on them. He pulled one of the boxes down and sat it on the floor to see what was behind it.

Peanut let out an intense bark. He gazed down at the box, which looked like it had been previously opened and taped shut.

"What do we got going on here?" He reached down and pulled the tape.

"Kenyon, what is your position? We've got a car going slowly by through the alley." The voice on the other end was Daniel's.

He opened the box. Objects wrapped in cloth and hand towels. He pulled one out. A handgun. "Be advised. The guns are still here but in the kitchen storage room. They won't be hauled out in wooden crates. Look for them to be carrying boxes with food labels."

Boxes the size that were on the shelf would only hold handguns or broken-down long guns. There might be rifles hidden somewhere else, but there was no time to continue the search.

"Kenyon, find a hiding place. The car has stopped."

The officers outside would have to shift positions quickly. Chances were, the brothers would enter from the side door that led directly to the kitchen. There was no time to communicate that to the team. They all had spent time studying the blueprints and photos of the bowling alley.

After putting the box back in place, Kenyon glanced around and then hurried into the kitchen and out into a hallway. With Peanut close by his side, he ducked into the employee restroom. Peanut leaned against his leg. The dog was so well trained she'd know to remain quiet. He left the door slightly ajar and peered out. Though his view was limited, the dark hallway would conceal him as long as he stayed quiet and no one looked closely.

He wondered exactly what was going on outside, but radio communication at this point was not a good idea. He could guess at the sequence of events that had transpired since they'd found the guns behind the bowling lanes. Most likely, an employee was involved in the movement of the guns just like with the pizzeria. Though the guns would not likely be found behind the lanes, moving them to the storage room the day transport was planned would provide easy quick access. A kitchen employee would be able to do something like that after closing with relative assurance of not calling attention to his actions.

The outside door rattled then swung open. He heard slow, heavy footsteps. There was no way he could determine if the man who had just entered was Brandon or Hal. He only hoped that whoever was watching this entrance had gotten a clear view of who had just stepped inside.

The hushed tones of two men talking filled the silence.

Maybe it wasn't the brothers. No signal had been given by any member of the team watching the outside of the building to move in. Or maybe they just hadn't had a clear look at who had entered the building.

He had to find out.

After giving Peanut the signal to stay, he slipped out of

the restroom and pressed his back against the wall, working his way back to the kitchen entrance. The two men were inside the storeroom, and the door was open. He slipped behind the grill, peering above it to see if he could get a clear view of either man.

One man was standing sideways and the other had his back completely turned.

The one turned sideways pulled boxes from the shelves.

One of the men threw up his arms. "You do it your way then." He stomped out of the storeroom and through the kitchen. "I need to get those rifles."

For just a second, Kenyon had a clear view of the man leaving the storeroom. Hal Jones. Kenyon had memorized the photo of him in the report.

If he could get back to the bathroom and close the door, he would be able to radio the others without being heard. He continued to watch the other man, waiting for him to come into the light that the single hanging bulb in the storeroom provided.

The man finished pulling boxes from the shelves and lifted one of them up. He put it back down immediately. "Too heavy. Going to need a hand truck."

The man stomped out of the storeroom into the kitchen. Kenyon scrambled around to the far side of the grill so he wouldn't be seen. His heart pounded as he pressed against the grill. He'd gotten a look at the man's face. Brandon.

Both men had been armed with handguns. Kenyon pressed his radio and whispered, "Both brothers in the building. I'm going after Brandon." He pulled his gun.

Kenyon stepped out of the kitchen into the hallway that led to where the lanes were. Just as he reached to open the door, a single gunshot echoed through the space.

EIGHTEEN

Heart racing, Kenyon pressed against a wall as silence descended once again. There was no way to know who had fired the gun or if the bullet had hit its target. Could have been one of the brothers or a task force member had done the shooting.

He waited for a radio report or orders, but none came. His heartbeat thrummed in his ears, and he opened the door and peered out with a view of the bowling lanes. It appeared that no one was in the area.

He wanted these men taken in tonight. They were the reason he'd lost months of his life and put his sons through a nightmare no little boy should experience.

He moved to step out. A bullet whizzed past him. He plunged back into the hallway. Brandon had been hiding underneath where the pins were.

"What was that gunshot about?" Brandon shouted. "Where is my brother?" Brandon's voice got louder then softer. He was moving around the space.

Kenyon saw his chance. "He's most likely dead, Brandon. This place is surrounded. You should just give yourself up."

The silence that followed tore through Kenyon. He had to make a move, get a bead on where Brandon was. He leaned out into the open space with a view of the lanes. In the shadows on the far side of the space, he saw West lift his head slightly from where he crouched behind the bowling ball dispenser machine. Gus must be there with him.

He scanned the whole area. Brandon could be hiding behind the counter where people check out shoes.

Kenyon stepped out, taking cover beside a vending machine. "Come on, Brandon. It's over." He adjusted his grip on the gun as a bead of sweat trickled down his temple. A picture flashed through his mind of Raina and the boys.

From where he was, he watched as West moved in closer, hiding behind another ball dispensing machine. West was assuming Brandon was behind the counter as well.

A voice came from above on the mezzanine where the second-floor offices were. "Brandon, he's on your back."

West stood up and took a shot at Hal and then crouched back down.

Kenyon stepped out, ready to back up West. His gaze moved to the mezzanine where a thudding noise had emanated, but Kenyon couldn't see what had happened to Hal. He drew his attention back to the shoe checkout counter.

The sound of a door opening and closing reached his ears. Bandon had escaped.

The voices through the radio came one after another as Kenyon, West and Jenna moved toward the door with their weapons drawn.

"Suspect is in the parking lot."

"Sniper take your shot."

"Suspect tossed a flash bang. Too much smoke. Can't see anything."

The smoke was still thick when Kenyon stepped out the front door where Brandon had gone. It stung his eyes. He saw West, but not Jenna. "Did you fire that earlier shot?"

"Yes, I saw Hal up on the mezzanine," West said. "I missed and he hid."

But West's second shot had probably hit Hal.

More smoke cleared, and he saw Jenna.

"Maybe we can still catch his brother." He heard Jenna give Augie the command to apprehend, and they disappeared into the smoke.

Kenyon headed back into the building to check on the status of Hal as the radio exchange continued.

"I think I see him running down the alley by the convenience store." That sounded like the guy staked out in the apartment building.

"We're in pursuit." Jenna's voice came through the speaker.

Kenyon spoke into his radio. "Be advised. He's armed."

Kenyon watched the mezzanine with his gun drawn. Had Hal been killed or just injured? He moved up the stairs. He found Hal's body behind an open door. When he checked for a pulse, there was none.

Inside the office, half a dozen rifles lay on the desk.

When he stepped back out, Daniel and Dakota were down below, standing at the end of one of the lanes.

"Hal is dead," said Kenyon.

"I'm sorry to hear that, but glad that his time as a criminal is over," said Daniel. "It'll be a good night if we can take in Brandon too."

Another voice came over the radio. "We've lost him. Suspect appears to have gotten into a car. No sign of him anywhere."

Daniel spoke into his radio. "Did you witness him get into a vehicle?"

"No."

"Search the area thoroughly. Let's not give up just yet." Daniel's shoulders slumped.

Kenyon tried to shake off the heavy sense of despair. It looked like Brandon had gotten away.

"It was still a good night," said Daniel. "The team worked well together."

"Maybe with Hal gone Brandon will get careless, since it was clear he wasn't the brains behind all this."

"Maybe," said Daniel.

Kenyon hurried down the stairs and into the bathroom where Peanut waited for him. She rushed into his arms, and he nuzzled his face against her soft ears. "Good girl. It's over for now."

Kenyon had only one thing on his mind. To get to Raina and the boys as quickly as possible and hold them in his arms.

He pulled out his phone to give Raina a call and tell her what had happened. He longed to hear the voice that gave him so much comfort.

Because the team needed to debrief after the stakeout, Raina had decided to ride in with Trish to meet Kenyon at the station. Though it was past midnight, she wanted to see Kenyon as soon as possible. The longing to be with him was almost overwhelming. The twins must have picked up on her restlessness. Though she'd put them down for bed, they really hadn't gone to sleep.

The sky was dark but filled with twinkling stars when they pulled into the PCPD parking lot. Still in his car seat, Trish lifted a sleeping Gabriel out of the back seat.

Raina unbuckled both the boys and helped them get out of the car. "Come on, guys. Let's go see Daddy." She held

Beacon's hand and Austin grabbed his brother's as they hurried into the building.

Trish pushed the code that would get them into the non-public part of the police station. They walked over to the elevator and rode it up to the third floor. Trish's phone pinged.

"A text from West. They are almost done with the debriefing."

They stepped out into the hallway and sat down on the benches outside the conference room. West was the first to come out of the room. He rushed over and gathered Trish into his arms. They walked off to a private space to be alone, with West carrying Gabriel in his car seat.

Jenna, Zach and Lucy exited the conference room. They both looked tired as they headed up the hallway toward the elevator.

Beacon tugged on Raina's sleeve. "When's Daddy coming out?"

"Soon. He had an important job to do tonight, so it might take him a little longer."

Raina sang the boys a song to entertain them. Austin crawled into her lap and Beacon leaned against her. They started to nod off.

The elevator doors opened, and a woman stepped out with an Australian shepherd wearing a K-9 vest. The dog was black and white with a hint of tan around his jowls and eyes. The woman was muscular and tall. Her blond hair covered her ears in a messy bob. "Excuse me, I'm looking for ATF agent Daniel Slater," she whispered.

Both boys had fallen asleep.

Raina pointed up the hall. "He's in a conference right now. They should be done shortly."

"Guess I'll wait." The woman took a chair not too far from Raina. The dog sat at her feet. "It was a long drive up from Bison Valley. I had duties to deal with into the evening."

The woman wore a US marshal's uniform.

"Are you part of the task force?"

"I'm about to be. Daniel's text said they had a big break in the case tonight."

"Yes. One of the brothers is no longer a factor."

"Are you married to one of the officers on the task force?"

Raina opened her mouth to explain but instead just said, "No."

Kenyon and Daniel came out of the conference room at the same time. Raina could feel the electric charge of Kenyon's gaze. She was pinned down by sleeping boys and couldn't move.

The US marshal had risen to her feet and stepped over to where Kenyon and Daniel stood. Her K-9 followed beside her.

She held out her hand to Daniel. "Lorelai Danvers."

"Glad you made it." Daniel turned to face Kenyon. "Lorelai replaces the US marshal we lost when she decided to go into witness protection."

"Yes, I remember reading about US Marshal Gracie Fitzpatrick's departure in the reports." Kenyon glanced in Raina's direction. He had official duties to take care of, but it was clear he wanted to rush over to her.

Raina's heart fluttered when he looked her way.

"Bixby is trained in tracking, which could prove to be an asset in the case." Daniel reached down to pet the Australian shepherd.

Kenyon's complete focus was on Raina as a soft smile spread across his face. "Ah, yeah, sure."

Daniel seemed to pick up on what was going on. He

clapped Kenyon's shoulder then looked in Raina's direction. "I'll let you go. Good work out there tonight." He addressed Lorelai. "Why don't you come into the conference room? I'll get you up to speed before you head over to your hotel. You got the voucher I sent you, right?"

"Yes," said Lorelai.

They disappeared into the conference room.

Kenyon hurried over to Raina and kneeled to be at her eye level. "What a night, huh?"

She lifted a hand to touch his cheek. The longing to be closer to him made her lean forward.

Austin stirred in her arms and spoke in a dreamy voice. "Daddy."

"We should get these two guys home and in their own beds, huh?"

Raina wondered what he meant by that. It seemed it would be abrupt and confusing to the boys if she went home to her house tonight. Plus, she needed to make sure it wasn't occupied. "Should I maybe stay one more night and then we can talk to the twins in the morning?"

A change in emotion flickered across Kenyon's face. "Yes, that would be good." His tone was flat.

Had he changed his mind about them trying out dating?

"Their car seats are downstairs."

"I'll help get them loaded and then go get Peanut out of the kennel."

Kenyon gathered a floppy, sleeping Beacon into his arms.

Daniel came out of the conference room with Lorelai behind him. He was holding his phone. His face had drained of color.

"I'm glad you're still here. I have some bad news."

Kenyon nodded. Raina stood up, holding Austin. "Is it okay if I hear this?"

"I think you should since it will affect you because of your close ties to Kenyon. Brandon just sent me a threatening message, probably from a burner phone. He has vowed revenge on the task force for his brother's death."

"That means all our lives are under threat," said Kenyon.

Raina tensed, causing Austin to stir in her arms. If they ended up together, this is what it meant to be married to a law enforcement officer. She had accepted that. At least the twins' lives were no longer under threat.

"I've sent a message to the group text. The whole team needs to be on red alert. We know how dangerous Brandon can be."

Kenyon nodded. "I've got to get these guys home."

"Take care," said Daniel. "Lorelai and I will escort you guys out just to be on the safe side."

They made their way downstairs and out to the patrol car. Daniel had treated her as if she was involved with Kenyon.

After they got the boys settled in their car seats, Daniel and Lorelai waited outside the patrol car while Kenyon went to retrieve Peanut.

She sat in the dark car listening to the sound of the twins breathing, wondering what the look on Kenyon's face meant. What was he going to tell her when they finally got a moment alone?

NINETEEN

Though Daniel had given the entire team permission to come into work an hour later, Kenyon got up early. He'd slept like a rock as soon as his head hit the pillow, though toward morning racing thoughts had caused him to wake up.

He padded softly down the hall and into the kitchen to put the coffeepot on. The news about Brandon's threat was disturbing, but it was not what had caused his mind to go a hundred miles an hour as morning light streamed through his window. He knew everyone on the task force would have each other's backs.

Last night when he could have died, he'd come to a realization. Life was too short to not take risks. Raina had just lived through the second worst thing the spouse of a police officer can experience, a long night of wondering if he would come home. The only thing worse was when the officer didn't come home due to being killed in the line of duty. Had the experience changed her feelings for him?

He poured a cup of coffee, leaned against the kitchen island and stared out the window, where early morning light washed over him and warmed his skin. He took a sip of the warm liquid, hearing feet padding behind him. When he turned, Raina stood in the doorway. Her long red hair framed her face, though her green eyes were dull with fatigue.

"You're up early."

"Couldn't sleep. Put some coffee on if you want some."

She moved over to the coffeepot and poured herself a cup. She turned to face him. "Will we have time to talk to the boys before you go to work about me moving out?"

He sat his coffee cup down. "I don't want you to move out."

"What are you saying? We can't go back to the way it was. We agreed about that."

He stepped toward her, pulled her coffee cup from her hand and sat it on the counter. "I don't want to try dating."

She angled her body slightly away from him. "I had a feeling you would just break my heart."

"No, Raina, that's not what I'm saying. You've been so patient about my indecisiveness."

She shook her head as tears formed in her eyes.

He put his fingers under her chin and turned her face toward him. "I don't ever want to be the cause of your tears again. Last night made me realize we don't need to date. That's just me being afraid to take a risk again. We've been friends long enough that I know who you are. I could have died last night, and I would never have gotten the chance to tell you I love you."

Her eyes brightened. "I love you too." A tear flowed down her cheek.

"You got to experience what it would be like to be married to a cop." He reached up and wiped the tear away with his finger brushing over her soft cheek.

"I thought about that too. I know that every time you step out that door, you might not come back. I accept that. It's worth the risk to spend my life with my best friend.

If you don't leap and take a risk, for sure you miss out on happiness."

"Well, best friend, I would very much like to marry you."

"Yes, Kenyon." She fell into his arms.

He held her for a moment then pulled back and kissed her. They pulled away but continued to gaze into each other's eyes.

"I want to marry you and be a mom to those two precious little boys."

A tiny voice came from the other side of the room. "See, I told you, Beacon. She does want to be our mom."

She turned to face the boys, who stood on the threshold of the kitchen with Peanut and Chewy by them, their tails wagging.

"Come here, you two." Kenyon and Raina both turned and bent down, opening their arms wide so Austin and Beacon could run into them. They stood together, each holding a child with their free arm wrapped around each other's back. Beacon wrapped his arms around Raina's neck and kissed her on her cheek.

"Mom," he said.

"Yes, yes indeed," she said.

Tears flowed again for Raina, but this time Kenyon was pretty sure they were happy tears. Joy burst through Kenyon. There was no other place he wanted to be but with the three people he loved the most in the world.

* * * * *

*If you enjoyed Kenyon's story, don't miss
Daniel's story next! Check out* Final Showdown
and the rest of the Dakota K-9 Unit series!

Chasing a Kidnapper
by Laura Scott, April 2025

Deadly Badlands Pursuit
by Sharee Stover, May 2025

Standing Watch
by Terri Reed, June 2025

Cold Case Peril
by Maggie K. Black, July 2025

Tracing Killer Evidence
by Jodie Bailey, August 2025

Threat of Revenge
by Jessica R. Patch, September 2025

Double Protection Duty
by Sharon Dunn, October 2025

Final Showdown
by Valerie Hansen, November 2025

Christmas K-9 Patrol
by Lynette Eason and Lenora Worth, December 2025

*Available only from Love Inspired Suspense
Discover more at LoveInspired.com*

Dear Reader,

I hope you enjoyed watching Raina and Kenyon face danger together as they learned to love each other in a deeper way. Kenyon is a man who has lost a great deal in his life, and it has made him afraid that more loss is just around the corner. After I got cancer, I found myself paralyzed with fear wondering what the next bad thing would be to happen to me. Even after the cancer was totally gone, I was bracing for more setbacks. This is no way to live. It is a given that, as long as we are here on planet Earth, loss and heartache will be a part of life. But I finally figured out that if I was going to fixate on trying to predict the next bad thing, I would miss celebrating all the good things I have in my life. You may be facing a loss right now. Let yourself feel the pain that loss has caused, but don't lose sight of all the good things God has brought into your life.

Sharon